PRAISE FOR *THE RAIN ASCENDS*

"This is the examination, powerful and disturbing, of weakness and depravity, of loyalty and love. Kogawa has written with quiet and solemn grace asking us to stretch our understanding beyond expected limits. When you close the covers of this book, it will not leave you behind." —*Ottawa Citizen*

"I deeply admire the tenaciousness of this work, and the risks it takes." —*The Globe and Mail*

"A work of art . . . The writing is like a globe of spun crystal." —*Toronto Star*

"Kogawa is at her best . . . A fascinating, troubling, and compassionate exploration of the dark side of human sexuality." —*Books in Canada*

"Kogawa [is] a writer of extraordinary compassion, understanding, courage, and grace." —*The Record* (Kitchener-Waterloo)

OTHER BOOKS BY JOY KOGAWA

Obasan

Itsuka

NOVEL FOR YOUNG READERS

Naomi's Road

POETRY

The Splintered Moon

A Choice of Dreams

Jericho Road

Woman in the Woods

THE RAIN ASCENDS

JOY KOGAWA

for Jill

blessings on your journey

Joy Kogawa

PENGUIN
CANADA

PENGUIN CANADA

Published by the Penguin Group

Penguin Books, a division of Pearson Canada, 10 Alcorn Avenue,
Toronto, Ontario, Canada M4V 3B2

Penguin Books Ltd, 80 Strand, London WC2R ORL, England

Penguin Putnam Inc., 375 Hudson Street, New York, New York 10014, U.S.A.

Penguin Books Australia Ltd, 250 Camberwell Road, Camberwell, Victoria 3124, Australia

Penguin Books India (P) Ltd, 11, Community Centre, Panchsheel Park,
New Delhi – 110 017, India

Penguin Books (NZ) Ltd, cnr Rosedale and Airborne Roads, Albany, Auckland 1310,
New Zealand

Penguin Books (South Africa) (Pty) Ltd, 24 Sturdee Avenue, Rosebank 2196, South Africa

Penguin Books Ltd, Registered Offices: 80 Strand, London WC2R ORL, England

First published 2003

1 3 5 7 9 10 8 6 4 2

Manufactured in Canada.

NATIONAL LIBRARY OF CANADA CATALOGUING IN PUBLICATION DATA

Kogawa, Joy
The rain ascends / Joy Kogawa.

ISBN 0-14-301320-3

I. Title.

PS8521.O44R35 2002   C813'.54   C2002-905505-9
PR9199.3.K63R35 2002

Visit Penguin Books' website at **www.penguin.ca**

"*Each of us must discover the secret key to
divine abandonment—that God has abandoned divine power
into the human condition utterly and completely,
so that we may not abandon each other.*"

ROSEMARY RUETHER

PROLOGUE

The town of Juniper, in the foothills of Alberta, celebrated the opening of the Juniper Centre of Music by declaring it C.B. Shelby Day after the founder of the centre, my father, the Reverend Dr. Charles Barnabas Shelby. Schoolchildren were given a holiday. Banners and balloons decorated the stores. The Shelby Family Quartet sang with the combined church choirs in a free concert in the shining new auditorium, and my brother, Charlie Junior, and I were the proudest children in town. The programme was heard later on Father's weekly radio broadcast, "Shelby Selects," and letters began to arrive enquiring about the Juniper Centre. Within five years, through our father's efforts, three new centres of music and healing were opened—one in Ontario, one in northern B.C. and a smaller one farther north.

✧   ✧   ✧

In the beginning is the fog, the thick impenetrable fog. The lie is the source of the fog and the lie is the fog. In the beginning there is also an unquenchable light. Everything in the house is touched by the fog and by light.

From within the density, this much alone is known: the way out of the lie is through mercy, the name of the path is mercy, the one who stoops to help is Mercy. Mercy's light is stronger than deception and betrayal, brighter than the most unspeakable abominations. Mercy will guide. She will circle the darkness and overcome it.

She came to me that spring in a dream and touched me in her evanescent way, saying that she, the Goddess of Mercy, was the Goddess of Abundance. Mercy and Abundance. One and the same. The statement shone in my mind with the luminosity of an altogether new moon.

What I am trusting, this pen-holding moment, is that it is she, the abundant and merciful one, who is both guide and transport for the journey. She is map, road and travelling companion, moving through light and shadow, dancing the direction. And what I realize just now for the first time is that it is not I on my own who seek her, but she who seeks me. It is she who in the act of flinging stones onto the forest floor—white stones, stepping stones, word stones—it is she who weaves the way towards herself. She draws me through the miasma of the day-by-heavy-day sad morning wakenings to her as yet unknown glad rising.

✧   ✧   ✧

The day you start out, the fog is so thick that when you open the window, it rolls into the room. Where the streetlight used

to be, there is only a fuzzy yellow blur. From the corner by the
bed comes the low growl of the cat, the fur on its back slowly
rising. You see her there, her green glowing eyes alert. You try
but you cannot close the window again. You back away. The
dampness invades with a hissing sound, flowing over the
calendar, the telephone, the desk, down to the floor. It rolls over
the cat and the green eyes blink and disappear. It attaches itself
to your skin and forms tiny droplets on the fine hairs of your
arms. It seeps into your pores. It moves softly, softly through
the keyhole and under the closed door.

Weariness.

You crawl along the moist floor, feeling for the desk legs, the
knobs on the drawers then up to the corner where the phone
sits ringing in the grey haze. You lift the receiver. You crouch
against the wall. You cannot speak. Eventually your hand grows
numb.

✧   ✧   ✧

Time without measure, in a Middle Eastern land called
Moriah, you are walking along, walking along, across the vast
stony plain and the blowing sand, past dry bones and scrub,
through storm and heat, obedient, faithful, into the dense fog,
carrying the fire and the knife.

You are Abraham, that patriarch, that trusting servant of
God, with a child, your son, the light of your life, walking
beside you, the firewood on his back, his soft child's hand in
your gnarled old hand.

"Father! Here's a pleasant stream. Shall we. . . ?"

"Why not, my boy."

This is Isaac by your side, the not-yet-strong, not-yet-powerful dreamer of your dreams, trusting but confused, trudging towards an altar where death and sacrifice are waiting.

"Isaac said to Abraham, 'Father,' and he answered, 'What is it, my son?' Isaac said, 'Here are the fire and the wood, but where is the young beast for the sacrifice?' Abraham answered, 'God will provide himself with a young beast for a sacrifice, my son.'"

It is innocent blood that is to be shed. You shield the child from the awful, the unspeakable truth. It's Isaac, your love, your laughter, your joy, your everything, who is the sacrificial lamb to be slain and offered to your ravenous God.

"And the two of them went on together and came to the place of which God had spoken."

Look how obedient I am. Look how I build the altar and arrange the wood, the kindling first, then the brush and the heavier branches on top—here and here, just so. And I take it apart and build it again. And again. And finally now, after all these years, because the wood is so dry, and the pyre is good enough, because I must get on with it, I bind him and lay him on the altar on top of the wood. I stretch out my hand. I take the knife and raise it high. And higher.

Where is the ram? Where in the bushes is the alternate sacrifice? Where is the voice that says, "Don't kill"?

My soul wails for direction. I walk the streets looking everywhere. I know the ram is there "caught in a thicket by his horns." If I hold the pen tight enough, with enough determination, if I let it fall just to the point—right up to the throat—that's when the ram will appear. I won't have to say the lethal words, will I?

I have enough faith to sit here in the fog by the phone, writing, not writing, telling, not telling. I have enough faith to try again, one more, one more time. I wait, the knife waits, the air sharp as earliest morning waits.

PART ONE

CHAPTER ONE

What Eleanor does not understand, what she refuses to understand, is that the truth is unspeakable. The truth is a knife that slays. That September night a year ago, when she called from Edmonton, she was as incoherent and hysterical as she had been the night before.

I could see her in one of her flouncy hippie skirts, standing in the hallway under the stairs of her rambling old house, her slightly masculine hand on her ample hips, her springy red hair more red than it used to be thanks to bottles of dye. Eleanor, my sister-in-law, was the bane of Mother's life, Mother's natural enemy, the thief who had stolen away in the night with her most precious possession, her son's heart. Eleanor thought to take one other son as well but that came later.

"My wife is clear about things, thank God," my brother Charlie says, "even if the rest of us aren't."

Eleanor is attached to us, grafted onto the family by marriage, but she is not "of" us. Her roots touch clearer water.

When the wind blows, she bends. Her branches do not break.

She pleaded with me as I sat there clutching the phone. "Talk to him," she said.

"I can't. I just can't. It was such a long time ago. Why *now?* What do you want of us, Eleanor? What do you want?"

Father is so very old, I was thinking, as we argued on again about whether Eleanor should come down to Ragland to talk to him herself. Dear God, isn't love enough? Isn't it enough that he loves us? I know he does. And I do love him. I've always loved him. Hundreds and thousands of people have had their lives brightened by him. Father's magic was the way he created gift boxes of time by creating events. He gave us life. Sparkling life.

"It's—it's just too unkind," I said finally. "He's so old. Can't we let him have some peace?"

"Peace!" Eleanor fairly shouted. "Oh yes! Peace! I'm all for it. How on earth can there be peace if we don't deal with this? Now! Before it's too late! It's not just for him, Mills. I know *I* need answers. I need the truth, for God's sake. Let's have some truth!"

"It's love," I said hesitantly, "I think it's love that's more important."

"You're wrong," she said. "Love without truth isn't love."

"I know they belong together, love and truth, but. . . ."

"Precisely," Eleanor interrupted. "They belong together. The thing is, you deny dignity when you deny responsibility. That's not love, Millicent. It's cowardice. He's not an idiot. He shouldn't be treated like one. He should know what he is. He's a—a criminal. A criminal!"

"Would you be happier if he was in prison? Who sends old men off to the front lines?"

"What front lines? I'm talking about responsibility. His. Yours too. And mine."

"Your responsibility? What responsibility could you possibly have?"

She was silent for so long that I thought the phone might have disconnected. Then her voice sounded choked as if she were trying not to cry. "Millie—God help us—if there's just one thing that history teaches us, just one thing—it's that bystanders and perpetrators are both on the same side."

It was my turn to say nothing as I held the receiver against my ear and sat rocking on my chair. God help us indeed, guilty bystanders that we all are—afraid to act, confused by the corruptions into which we are born. When it comes to Father, there's no denying whose side I was on at the time. If I was guilty of a crime, it was my heart that was indicted.

"I've tried to talk to him, Eleanor. I've really tried. But it's too late. It's just too late in the day."

"It's never too late," Eleanor said. "Truth is never too late for anyone."

"What on earth do we mean by truth? We can't possibly know what it means. It's like the sun shining on the other side of the world. It's beyond us."

"Then we have to walk to the other side of the world. That's what we have to do. Think of it as a quest for fire, Mills. You're the one right there. You're the closest person in his life. God knows he won't tell me anything."

"He won't tell me either."

"Yes he will. You've always been there for him. Oh God, you've been like—like Hitler's cat—if Hitler had a cat."

"Oh how absurd. Father is not Hitler."

"But all you do is mewl about love. Face the truth, for once, woman!"

I had not pictured myself as Hitler's cat, but if that was the way she saw me, if that was the way I was to be seen, then so be it, I thought. On the great judgement day, Hitler's cat can stand in front of that awesome cloud of witnesses and yowl its unacceptable tale of affection. Then all the people will scream and gnash their teeth as they cast it forth into eternal damnation along with the monster.

Eleanor can not know how much I loved Father, how much I have always loved him, in spite of every, every thing, in spite of everything. I am his one and only, loyal, devoted daughter.

A friend, they say, is someone who helps you hide the body. But Eleanor, my brother's strong-minded wife, was telling me to exhume the skeleton garbed in the robes of a priest—a skeleton busily hiding other small skeletons between the walls.

"God knows how many victims there were," Eleanor said. "Just stop for once in your life and think about *them*. The families. Consider the victims, for heaven's sake."

She was asking me to hear the wailing in the night, to consider the suffering I did not see, to consider another point of view. My reply was that these considerations were not my province. I was his child, his well-fed cat if you will, and I was witness for the defence. I was retained, before I was born, to be his advocate.

In the late-night courtroom of my thoughts, I heard her arguing that my mothering, surrounding, defending love was misplaced, and that I more properly belonged with the weak. But as I took my stand beside my father, beside and around, I declared that I knew of no criminal who was not also weak, not also a victim. It was only the mob of accusers who were invulnerable.

I tried to give her my perspective—a view from a lowly place beside a bowl of milk and a plate of table scraps. I told her I would leave it to his accusers to chronicle his crimes.

"You're wrong!" cried Eleanor's angry voice, her three a.m. telephone weeping voice. "Face the rage, Millie. Let it out before it eats you alive. For God's sake, let it out!"

"To whom, Eleanor? Let it out to whom?"

"To the bishop. Tell him. Write to him."

"But he's our friend! How could I possibly?" She could more reasonably have suggested I take off my clothes and run naked down the noonday street.

"Tell me, then. At least find out what the extent of it is."

So said Eleanor in the late night, but from within the fog I could think only that I had pledged my loyalty to my beloved father. In my lifetime of knowing him I had experienced such tenderness, such wisdom and kindness and forbearance, such gentle forgivingness and largeness of heart, that I was able, even with all that I knew, to utter the word *Father*, and to understand it as a metaphor for God. Father, God. Our Father, which art in heaven, hallowed be Thy Name.

We go to extreme lengths—we devoted daughters, we women, we children, we slaves of the men we love—we go to extreme lengths in our efforts to justify our unacceptable loyalties. We expend our days and nights thinking of ways to protect and redeem them.

Eleanor accuses me of constantly choosing the darkness. "You may be right," I said. "But people, so many people, see him as the soul of saintliness." Last Sunday in church, one woman remarked on his "spiritual aura" and said, "I've rarely seen that certain quality. He's so gentle. I feel closer here with him to that spiritual centre than anywhere else I have ever been." People say these things and I do not doubt their sincerity. I do not. My father, Eleanor, my father, dear people of the jury, is known to be a good man. And so help me, God, this is also true.

But Eleanor, who knows better, who knows worse, chants her mantra in my midnight ear: The truth, the truth, the hidden truth. Take the sword of truth and cut the knots. Then you'll be free.

The knots are in my bowels, Eleanor. A sword in the bowels is not usually there to make one free.

People go mad in these circumstances. Their minds unravel. As she drags me into the courtroom to take my stand, when I raise my hand and swear to tell the truth, the whole truth and nothing but the truth, I am stating what cannot be done. Yet she persists, my dear sister-in-law, she who is judge, jury and prosecutor, passionate for justice and health. The crime must be uncovered and the prisoner brought forth in his chains. This is required. Vindication for the victims. Vengeance even.

CHAPTER TWO

Once again, then, you are here at the impossible beginning, struggling with the fear that all that you love may yet be required. You are standing at the top of the creaky stairs in the long moment before diving. You begin the descent, one stumbling step after another. The act of beginning is the same act over and over, the half-crazed act with pages torn from the heart's walls and flung onto the debris-covered floor.

For almost as long as you can remember, you have been here, at the beginning, at the edge of knowing. You are like a racehorse at the starting line, pawing the track, the reins held too tight, too long. Your legs are too tense. A certain paralysis has set in. And now you are hearing the starting gun again, the sharp retort like a dull roar filtered through the background shouting of the crowd.

You are holding the bannister with both hands. Your body is as steady as you can manage. Down and down you are propelled in the greyness of pre-dawn. You are nearing the bottom of the stairs. Your heart is wild with resolve, your dangerous weapon of half-truths clutched tight in your shaking hand. You tell yourself you must use the instrument skilfully, you must make the incision as precisely as a surgeon, cutting carefully so that the nerve is not severed. You have donned your mask, your gloves. What is required is to see the face behind the face, the hideous face of Mr. Hyde that you know is there, but that you have not once, not ever, seen.

However strong your intention, you can only proceed with quaking heart and feeble prayer. You can see the light from the fireplace reflected in the dining-room mirror, dancing yellow and red and orange. He is there in front of the fire, this irreplaceable man whose blood is your blood, whose name is your name. Your reason for approaching him comes from him, your courage and cowardice come from him, your values come from him, and the judgement with which you judge him comes from him. Love comes from him.

The wonder of your father has always existed—the warmth, the tenderness. He was a god. In the beginning was the one who could do no wrong, the maker and keeper of all laws. With a wave of his hand he formed the land. The clinging mist that surrounded the house could not extinguish the light, the bravely flickering light. Now, in his old age, it continues to glow through the mist. You move towards it. You trust it still.

He is sitting by the fireplace, his body shrunken with age, his rounded back to you, his long fingers spread wide to the warmth. The logs are crackling softly in the stillness.

He is a mild and sensitive man, your father, but complex, intelligent and extraordinarily vital. He is larger than life. Even in his mid-eighties, he is larger than life. He weeps more, sings more, prays more, does more, than anyone I know. He is a man of immense appetites and immense contradictions, a man who is greatly admired and equally despised, a man of faith and a man of falsehood. The world has never been big enough for him, this saint and sinner combined. Each precious day was never long enough for all that he crowded into it.

I do not know how this man of great secrecy and great openness, this charismatic communicator and liar, this man who indulges himself, who sacrifices himself, who is utterly selfish and who magnanimously opens his house to strangers, this man who is guilty and seemingly as innocent as a cloud—I do not know how he survives the quicksand of his own paradoxical being.

He is crouched slightly forward on the leather elephant stool, his now stooped and fragile frame wrapped in the old wine velour bathrobe Mother gave him many Christmases ago. His face is roughly shaven, the long white brows untrimmed.

"You're up early." His morning voice is slightly rasping and he clears his throat. He reaches over to the coffee table to pick up his cup of tea.

"I couldn't sleep."

He doesn't respond. He may not have heard you. You repeat yourself. He would not want to know why you were up all night. He would want it all to go away. So would you. Yes. So would you. He would want you never to raise the matter again. He may be thinking of that spasm of a conversation yesterday, your failed effort to speak. He may sense that you are about to pounce on him again. His hand shakes as he lifts the cup of tea to his lips. The saucer contains a small brown pool that drips onto the rug.

You are waiting patiently for the right moment. "Patience," Mother used to say, "is a great virtue." And she was herself an extraordinarily patient person. About a decade ago, she was given a cutting from a night-blooming cereus, a strange, tropical cactus plant with foot-long narrow leaves. She tended it with great patience, saying that in ten years it would flower. But she died before she saw the fruits of her labour.

Mother was virtuous and stoical. She was good, but she was not fun. Father was the one you loved to be near. He was the one person in the entire world you loved and trusted the most. Years and years ago, when you first learned about the deep fissure in his life, you plastered it over with mud and wordlessness. But Eleanor's midnight storms have washed away the patchwork and the crack in the foundation of your heart lies deeply exposed.

If Father could have publicly confessed, if he could have faced the consequences and quit the church, you might have been able to walk down the road with him, with pity, with love. But that never happened.

It is your intention now to ask him what you were unable to yesterday, and to try again to broach the impossible subject. You, like Eleanor, need answers. You both need desperately to know.

"I couldn't sleep," you repeat a third time. You wait for a comment, but he says nothing. You can feel the pressure, a visceral force within you as you prepare to leap. You clear your throat. In that instant he shifts. His head turns slightly. The lines beneath his eyes are dark and puffy—a heavy sadness. He begins to stand, faltering slightly. His hand shakes as he pushes himself off the stool, then he steadies himself on the arm of the chesterfield. One slippered step to the side and he totters upright. He begins his slow shuffling race away from you, towards the dining room, his study/bedroom, past the much tethered night-blooming cereus, which now reaches the ceiling.

You watch his retreat. The first opportunity of the morning is disappearing. You will have to wait, you tell yourself. He won't die between now and noon. You will wait until lunchtime. When you sit down to eat, you will try again.

You stay in the living room, leaning back on the couch, watching the sky grow light. Then you notice, on the fireplace hearth and in the ashes, the bits of paper, corners of envelopes, one red ribbon curled like a comma, a half-burnt punctuation mark. It doesn't occur to you until later that he may have been destroying the evidence.

CHAPTER THREE

You can sometimes go for days without thinking about it. Or if you do, briefly, you sweep the thought aside, quietly under the carpet with the undisturbed dust of other imponderables, other better forgotten small burials, insect wings.

But then the TV is turned on and the news report tells another story. V, these media-mangled days, is for victim and, yes, sweet vengeance.

There was a time when the sky was so full of geese flying north, or geese flying south, that they stretched in the longest V from one end of the earth to the other. V for victory. Remember those days? Remember the time when people loved him, followed him, flocked to him? V today is for vortex in a sky of non-existent birds. The ghosts of tiny songbirds fly through fields sprayed with pesticides.

I can imagine another kind of V—a jagged V with Father at the head of a long descent, leading us all downwards, and we're tied together on either side of him by long ropes knotted around our waists as we follow him into the caverns, into light-lessness, into the slippery, cold underground. Somewhere in the sunlight the rope is strapped around the base of a merciful tree. Somewhere in the air birds are flying to a warm country. V is for velocity.

V is also for voracious, which is the most accurate word for Father. He was born that way.

"Oh yes, he was a hungry one," Grandmother Shelby said of Father.

I was fourteen years old when I first visited Grandmother Shelby in that beautiful "sceptred isle" of my ancestors, land of hope and glory, Buckingham Palace and "Turn again Whittington, thrice Lord Mayor of London." It was like walking into my nursery rhymes, and dear old Granny Shelby was Mother Goose, lacy in shawls, her ample arms smelling of ginger cookies.

On her crowded mantelpiece lived her far-flung family, Charlie and me as babies, Father as a child with his two older brothers, all three in cloth caps and darned stockings and boots and knickerbockers, and my assorted cousins and great-grandparents, an uncle who was at Dunkirk. I loved the photo-graphs and Father's first trumpet that belonged to Granny's brother and the stream in the village and the woods and the pub with its dartboard, and the graveyard at the church—all the names and the stories, all the centuries of who we have been.

"I'd say, Millicent, child, that you take after the Shelby side," Granny said one day. I was blissfully unaware of any imperfections in the Shelby side and was pleased. She showed me a small sepia photograph of herself as a young woman in a bonnet and told me we both had her father's cheekbones—rather prominent cheekbones.

That photograph sits these days in its silver frame on the top, right-hand corner of Father's holy of holies, his rolltop desk. One of the rules in our house was that Father was not to be disturbed when he was at his desk. Mother told me years ago that she never even touched the handle of the study door when it was closed. I have wondered in recent years whether the desk is Father's shrine to midnight, whether somewhere, behind the shelf of diaries, he keeps his portrait of Dorian Gray or his potion for Dr. Jekyll and Mr. Hyde. I don't know, of course, since I've never seen inside the desk.

Who knows what secrets from its dark corners he may have been burning in the fireplace this morning. While I was talking with Eleanor last night again, Father could have been furtively sorting through papers, destroying letters, trying to conceal the small bones, bones, all those little bones scratching about in the night, keeping me awake.

How many men there must be, like Father, who have become heroes by excising their villainies from their stories. How many autobiographies are monuments to half-truths, masking the multifaceted bundles of imperfection that we all are? Ah Father, we live in a world where criminals are in the pulpits and saints are in prison and the children of the future live in boxes on the streets. You have been walking for so long in a light so bright it fills me with awe and in darkness so deep it makes me gasp. I don't know how you live with yourself, or what made you this way.

People are inclined to blame parents for their children's misdemeanours. But it has never occurred to me to think of Granny Shelby as the source of Father's troubles. She was warmth and laughter, her rolling chuckles as comforting as England's mild summer air.

"Come feed the scraps to the birds, my love. Come see the birds in their bath."

I loved Granny and her little house from which we could watch the small robins and the rabbits hopping across the moist green fields, and the sheep rounding the corner of the village street. What little I know of Father's infancy has come from late-afternoon conversations with Granny Shelby. We sat with our tea and sandwiches in trays while the sun silently climbed the walls and the old dog lolled in front of the fire.

"You mustn't tell anyone this," she confided once, leaning towards me conspiratorially, "but your father was my favourite child."

The planet, she said, had a habit of spewing forth its prize babies every so often. In a litter of pups there is always one that is larger and more energetic than the rest, its eyes opening first, its tail wagging faster. And so too, among humans, there are special children. One finds them in unexpected places—in slums among garbage-eaters or dressed in silks or floating in baskets among reeds. "It's random. Like winning the football pools. And your father was dropped down, my lovely jackpot baby, out of that beautiful southern sky and into my arms."

They were in India at the time he was born. She held a photograph of him in a white frilly dress, a toddler in his mother's arms, his curly blond head against her bosom. For Grandmother Shelby, Charles Barnabas was the perfect child, the one who could do no wrong.

Baby boys dressed as girls do not grow up confused, I've read. On the contrary, the more tenderly they are treated the stronger they become. I have searched and sifted through Granny's stories but find no clues, unless it was that Granny

Shelby needed Father to be more special than he was, unless the ordinary rules did not apply.

"He was eager from the beginning," she said. "His eyes. Oh my. Deep and dark and hungry as the jungle. You could see right away—this one was a personage."

He was the third of her three boys, and the only one to be born in India, where Grandfather Shelby was teaching. "My youngest hatched naked in the tropics and feathered in England." Little Charles Barnabas was barely toilet-trained when the fourth Shelby baby was stillborn, and Father, at the age of three, suckled the extra breast milk on board the ship that took the family back to the old country.

"What a sailing!" Granny's eyes were twinkling. "Our Charles Barnabas and the ladies holding their parasols over him while he read. . . ." The story spread among the passengers that here, from the Shelby household, was a bright young 'un. Before they docked in Southampton, he had succeeded in enthralling the entire ship by reading aloud from old copies of *Punch* and the *London Illustrated News*. "Not that he could understand all the words, mind you, but he could read better than the bigger boys."

He was always in the "A" stream and at the top of his form. He could act, sing, write, and he won every essay contest in the school. It can't have been easy for Father, always the youngest and brightest and therefore a target for bullying. It can't have been easy for any of the Shelbys after their return to England. Grandfather, who had been ill, died. The family was destitute.

Granny had little to tell me about their years of poverty or the way Father as a youth suddenly disappeared from her life. "Oh I don't know," she said and her voice trailed away. "It wasn't an easy time." Three years after Grandfather's death she herself became ill and the boys were cared for by a spinster aunt. "She didn't understand children," Granny said. "I should not have let her take them." "How old was Father?" I asked. She had a faraway look as she rubbed her abdomen and her cup of tea grew cold. "Oh about seven or eight."

Father was barely fourteen when he left for India with a magistrate who had become from time to time the family benefactor. As Granny described it, her Charlie B. fell from poverty through the looking glass into wonderland. "It was all very posh on board," Granny said. Posh stood for "port outbound, starboard homebound." Coming or going, the wealthy sailed on the shady side of the ship.

Father was hired to tutor a diplomat's child for the summer. He was expected to return home for the school term, but he was captured by India, land of his birth and pampered infancy. He followed mystics, gurus and storytellers, he sang, danced, walked, talked and wandered throughout the east, returning to the magistrate's home for refuelling and at other times working as office clerk and shipper in a British trading company, until his restless feet felt the lure of the North.

It was in Alaska, land of the long sub-zero nights, that Father first encountered the Light of Life. Father has told this story from the pulpit so many times I can remember it almost word for word. It was the major turning point of his life. "There was I in the snows and the cold, romancing the north and prancing about with a heart that wouldn't keep an old dog alive, when I was brought face to face with my Conqueror." He was by nature, he said, a spiritual man, but he was not religious in the conventional sense. When it came to Christianity, he'd had an open mind. Unlike the writer C.S. Lewis, who was dragged kicking into Christianity, Father was wafted in through a sea of delirium.

Late one constantly twilight night, Father collapsed and was taken to hospital. He realized with a certain luminous clarity that he was facing the ultimate crisis. As his final conscious act, he moved to locate himself in relation to the Unfathomable. As he lay a heartbeat away from death, he forced himself to sit up and pray. He remained in an attitude of prayer for the next three months, focussing his attention on a painting on the opposite wall of Jesus as a twelve-year-old in prayer. During this entire time, his faulty heart was expected to stop at any moment.

One late afternoon, as he prayed, the wall was no longer there. Instead he looked out onto a vast field. He became aware of a tiny dot in the distance. Almost at the instant of that awareness, almost as a flash of lightning, the dot sped towards him and there, in a burst of incandescent light, with his arms loosely at his sides, palms up, his head gently inclined, was the Christ.

Father tried to cry out, "My Lord." He tried to lift his arms. But he could do nothing and the vision vanished. He was suffused with an awe and a rapture beyond words—an overwhelming joy, a great rushing fire and wind in his mind. The following day his heartbeat was normal. He was the talk of the hospital. "A miracle," the doctors said.

From the moment of his healing, Father was seized with a sense of divine mission. "I, who had fled to the ends of the earth, to the south and to the east, to the west and to the north, I was caught and gently thereafter held in the loving jaws of the Hound of Heaven." His life, he said, no longer belonged to him.

That story was the first of several miracle tales. As a child, I did not then, nor do I now, doubt the authenticity of his experiences. They were the signs of his authority. Like St. Paul, who encountered the Lord on the road to Damascus, Father too had met the One who saves.

Over his decades of ministry, Father has been showered with rare spiritual blessings. He has been cured of numerous illnesses, rescued from many dangers.

One winter he was driving alone on a country road and was caught in the middle of wildly swirling snow, the worst blizzard of the year. As he told it later, the road disappeared. There were no other cars at all and, with the wind-chill factor, the temperature was about forty below. He knew he couldn't survive for long, stuck in the ditch in a stalled car that was rapidly being buried.

Once more he had been brought to death's door. He sat for a while in the growing numbness, praying, handing himself over to the peace and guidance of God. From within the peace, he began to sing with increasing joy a hymn of praise. Then, once more, in the distance, a tiny light. He followed it and came upon a hut where a man peered out at him from a frosty window and would not let him in.

"But praise God," Father cried. "Praise God. He knew what had to be done. He came out and rubbed my hands and face with snow and saved my life."

As a child, I listened to his endless personal stories of a loving, protecting, healing God. He was the Great Fisherman's own fisherman. I witnessed his faithful devotions. I accompanied him on his hospital rounds and saw the old and the sick weeping in his arms. He brought peace to the dying, his eyes raised in petition.

His love of people and his service continue to this very hour. Yesterday, for example, around three in the afternoon, he suddenly felt compelled to pick up the phone and call old Mrs. Jensen who had been seriously ill. He told me he was anxious to visit her. He insisted it had to be right away. It was quite a long way out in the country, but I got directions from her son and we went. That was our second visit with the sick yesterday. Earlier we'd gone to the hospital.

Mrs. Jensen's eyes were closed when we came in, her mouth open in a rapid laboured breathing. Father sat beside her, held her hands and wept silently.

"Oh God, you have given us eternal life. Bless your dear child, Viola Jensen. . . ."

His prayer was a direct and clear communication with the God of love, in whom my father trusts.

"Thank you, my dear dear friend," she managed to gasp between breaths.

We returned home. A few hours later the phone call came saying she had died peacefully.

"Yes," Father whispered, his face infinitely gentle.

It's gentleness that most defines him now in his old age, and it's gentleness, I'm told, that marks the presence of a saint. All the forces of darkness cannot rob him of an essential kindness. All the judgement of people cannot blot out his deeds of love. His faith is genuine. Two of us in this world have known the truth of this in great detail. And now that Mother is gone, I may be the only one left to bear witness, the only one left to serve and protect him in his vulnerable and fragile old age.

CHAPTER FOUR

"A good man," Mother used to say in her increasingly senile years. "Barnabas is a good man." Those were the last words she said to Father before she died. There is not the slightest doubt in my mind that she loved him faithfully, unswervingly, down the tortuous path of many betrayals to the very end.

It was late in the Advent season last year, during a heavy snowfall, that the steadfast tin soldier with her permanent lean was finally swept away. Father and I had been out Christmas shopping. We came in to find her asleep on the couch, the TV on, a children's choir singing "O Holy Night." It wasn't until he tried to waken her for a cup of tea that we discovered she was gone.

She left us surrounded by the sounds and sights of the most family-centred season. The tree, not to be decorated until Christmas Eve, was still naked and fragrant by the piano. Early in December, she'd watched the gradual arrival of the annual deluge of cards. Hundreds, literally hundreds, of Christmas

cards had been arriving, as they did every year, and were standing in increasingly tight formation along the mantelpiece,
hiding the crystal vase and the three bronze monkeys who see,
hear and speak no evil. As Advent proceeded, the cards spilled
onto the bookcases, the buffet, the sideboard, the window
ledges, and finally they dangled as rows of streamers tacked
around the dining room. A somewhat gaudy display but proof
enough that the Shelby family was well loved.

At Easter there would still be as many as usual—cards with
long personal letters from Father's still active network of
friends, colleagues, devotees. "My dear Shelby." "Dear Father
Charles Barnabas." And a few late sympathy cards. "We're so
sorry to hear that Mrs. Shelby is no longer with us." "May you
be comforted in your loneliness at this holy Easter season."

Mother's last words were spoken as she held Father's hands.
"Barnabas is a good man." She was paraphrasing Scripture,
referring to the Book of Acts, where Barnabas, "son of conso-
lation," is tersely described in chapter eleven, verse twenty-four.
"Barnabas was a good man."

That is all we are told of Barnabas. That is all Mother
allowed herself to know about Father. He was good. And so
amen and amen—let it not be denied, and let the simple words
be engraved on his tombstone when the time comes that his
grandchildren's grandchildren may know that whatever else is
remembered of the Reverend Dr. Charles B. Shelby, servant of
God, he was also a good man.

I can hear Eleanor's impatience as I align myself with
Mother and continue to paint him in perfect pastel. But to
focus solely on "the evil that men do" is surely equally flawed
as a way of perceiving reality. As Hitler's cat, am I not entitled

to say that Hitler was human too, that he had some moments of kindness?

One request, Eleanor—that I may stay for a while in the light, his brilliant light—that I may drink once more from our fountain of song and linger a few moments longer in a happiness I once knew. Then after that, I will come softly into the darkness. I will see with my night blindness, with my body turned to acid, I will see then what I cannot yet see. Something grotesque. Something to be removed, violently if necessary, from our midst.

✧   ✧   ✧

"Defend O Lord, *this* Thy child with Thy heavenly grace."

The bishop's hands rested on my head as they did on the head of each child presented for confirmation. But I could feel the special pressure on my temples as I knelt before him, and the warmth as he pressed down and intoned the words in a rich deep voice that filled the church, ". . . that she may continue Thine forever. . . ." At this moment the grace of God and the power of the Holy Spirit were being poured into my life.

There were about ten of us, aged twelve to fourteen, walking up one by one to the railing, the girls in white dresses. But only I was the rector's daughter, only I was known personally by the bishop. His hand had a large ruby ring. Everything about the bishop was large, his voice, his oversized head with its wobbly jowls. He had a round, protruding belly that you could see under his cassock.

Father in contrast was thinner and taller. Instead of jowls, he had hollow cheeks and a slightly scraggly dark beard. But his

voice was as strong as the bishop's. The two together were
louder than the entire choir.

The day of my confirmation was only one of many magical
days, the congregation babbling, dainty sandwiches being
passed around on silver trays and Mother, regal as usual in her
wide-brimmed white hat, pouring tea at the long table on the
lawn in front of the church. But always it was Father who drew
the crowds—Father with his head flung back, slapping his
thigh as he shouted at some joke.

In all my life I experienced no rudeness or coarseness of any
kind between Father and Mother. I was raised so carefully, so
piously, so properly, raised not to swear or to think unseemly
thoughts.

"There are two kinds of people in the world," Father used to
say to Charlie and me. "Those who belong to royalty and those
who do not. 'Cast not your pearls before swine,' children. Be
careful when you speak, not to trample on what people say, and
don't belittle others. Above all, be kind. That is the sign of
royalty. Look for pearls in whatever is being said. Royalty has
the power to turn dung into pearls. Swine turn pearls into
dung." Father had the capacity to turn the world's many small
unkindnesses into lessons and gifts from God.

"He has such a generous heart," Mother would say admir-
ingly.

Father truly was a much loved and popular priest and, as a
result, our family had a great deal of prestige. His use of the
word "royalty" had the added and perverse effect of making me
feel above it all. We were the perfect, the model family in
communities of people not quite our peers. We were, after all,
the Shelby family—as in the Shelby Family Quartet, heard

every Sunday singing the theme for Father's Sunday broadcast.

On the air and off the air, Father was a total communicator. Was, I say, in the past tense, when in fact he still is one of the most connected people I know. His daily correspondence even today confounds the postman.

"That's quite a load you get, sir."

"Fish need water," I told the postman, "birds need air, Father needs people. He breathes people."

Father's appetite for conversation is immense. His white priestly collar catches the eyes of strangers who sometimes seek him out hoping for a word of comfort. They are not often disappointed. He listens. He advises.

"If you weep with those who weep," he says, "you diminish their burdens by half. If you rejoice with those who rejoice, you double their joy." He practises this creed and he has more visitors than anyone I know.

Back in my childhood Father was connected to people from as far away as Australia. Their voices arrived in pocketbook-size boxes of wire which Father played on his Webster Chicago wire recorder, that imperfect machine with its wavery sound and its nest of wires becoming unsprung. Wire gave way eventually to tape. We had broadcast-quality tape recorders, all sizes of tape recorders. Father indulged himself in the latest communication technology—movie cameras, still cameras, projectors, duplicating machines. Charlie and I were the envy of our chums as we paraded them into the crowded studio library to watch home movies, to record plays. We rigged up a microphone and pretended to be radio broadcasters. I was frequently the sound person, slamming doors, pouring water into glasses, stamping my feet to announce arrivals.

Once Father brought home a heavy rectangular beige case which he said was a Wilcox Gay contraption for making records—thin, bendable, shiny black records. The Shelby family found their singing way in a package of records to a real radio station and Father's life as a broadcaster followed not long after.

The day of Father's first programme, I stood on one leg after the other in my excitement, glowing in the glory of our new-found fame. Mother and Charlie too, their faces bright, stood in front of our fancy black radio as we added our soprano, alto and tenor voices to our radio voices and sang our proud hearts out.

I love to tell the story
Of unseen things above. . . .

Mother said it was the music that first attracted her to Father. They were two singing pilgrims from England who had followed their destinies to meet on the Salvation Army snowy streets beneath the magical northern lights. Meredith Hunter, Anglican deaconess, stood in her parka under a flickering sky on the edge of a small northern crowd, enchanted by the trumpet-playing street preacher. He caught a glimpse of her golden hair and heard her clear soprano voice.

"I thought she was an angel from heaven."

They were married after a long and tortuous engagement that spanned nearly a decade while they wrestled their way through denominational differences. Eventually Father bowed to Mother's convictions. He studied for the high calling—the Anglican variety.

My brother, Charlie Junior, the golden boy, was their first child. Six long years and one miscarriage later came me, the not-very-pretty sister with stick-out teeth, slightly tan-toned skin and thick, dark, curly hair. It seems that somewhere back in my father's line there had been a "Black Norwegian."

Except for my teeth, I was proud to be who I was, a well-mannered daughter of a Church of England clergyman and his wife—his perfect wife. That was the one thing everyone could agree on. Mother was perfect. She was dignity and elegance and reserve, the quintessential clergy wife, keeping the exact balance between kindness and distance that commanded complete respect. She did not engage in small talk or gossip, either at home or in company. She was as faultless a person as I have ever known—too faultless perhaps for regular folks. She had no confidantes among her friends.

For most of my childhood we lived in and around Juniper, Alberta, not far from Mother's younger brother, Uncle Jack, who like many other European pioneers had come from the old country, lured by the CPR's offer of free land. Uncle Jack was completely different from Mother—a rather rowdy man. Apart from ourselves, there were a few other English families, some Germans and Poles, a large contingent of Ukrainians, some Mennonites from Russia, some Americans. One girl's austere father had come from Iceland. A boy who wore suspenders had parents who grew up in Wales.

One time in grade four, the teacher asked each child about the work our fathers did. I counted one mechanic, one grain elevator worker, the postmaster, the lumberyard manager. Almost all the others were farmers or farm workers or ranch hands. The most defiant boy in the class said, "I don't got a dad."

When it was my turn to stand and speak, the whole class, even the prettiest and most popular girl, looked up at me enviously. My father was the best educated and the best known and we, the singing Shelbys, were clearly at the top of the Juniper social heap. Our home, the Anglican rectory, had an Encyclopedia Britannica set, *Life* magazines, a piano, lace curtains and everything one could dream of. We set the standards. Even the notes Charlie and I brought to the teachers were properly sealed in envelopes, unlike the folded pieces of paper other children clutched in their fists.

Charlie and I together won so many awards and badges and certificates that we hardly had enough space on our walls to display them. Music awards, scholastic awards. Mother was never excessive in her approval, simply smiling, or more often nodding, when we'd return from school in triumph with some show of honour. Father however was more jubilant than either Charlie or me.

"That's my girl," he'd say proudly, admiring my prize. I lived for those moments of praise. I tried to outdo Charlie, my only competitor. One year Charlie won the all-round student award. I thought he was insufferable, removing all the ornaments over the fireplace and placing his trophy in the centre.

As older brothers go, however, Charlie was not bad. He was a bit pompous and wordy, but he was well liked by the teachers. "So like his father," they would say. Charlie walked like Father. He talked and laughed like him, throwing his head back and opening his mouth wide to the sky. But at home the lines were drawn differently. Charlie was Mother's child. I aligned myself with Father. Like him, I got things done quickly. Charlie and Mother were slow and methodical.

Father and I were always in the car first and waiting for the dawdlers.

"You two are the 'leap-before-you-look' types," Mother would say. "It will get you both into trouble."

Charlie was not just temperamentally like Mother, he also had her fair skin and blue eyes. "Blue as the prairie sky," one parishioner said. Father and I were darker. Although she never said it outright, I felt Mother thought it a pity that my colouring was what it was. Uncle Jack once mumbled something about "a touch of the tar" but Mother turned quickly aside and said, "She has beautiful eyes, Jack, beautiful dark eyes like her father. She's so much like him." That was fine by me.

I worshipped Father. He was funny and enthusiastic as a puppy. He joked easily. He cried easily. All the rich and colourful stuff of life flowed through him. He would come into a gloomy room with his buoyant good humour and the shadows would vanish. Mother said, "He carries problems as if they're sunbeams."

Life was one ongoing special event from Easter morning egg-hunts to summer camps, Christmas pageants, young people's parties, picnics, concerts, fund-raising dinners, teas and bazaars. And our home was a turbulent river, overflowing with stories, songs, feastings. There were always people around—people with their triumphs and tragedies and intimacies, coming and going to meetings, counselling sessions, in and out of one crisis or another—people getting married or buried or just dropping in for tea. During the busy Juniper Centre years when Father was also rural dean, Mother, Charlie and I would get in the Austin A40 with Father and drive to the several outlying hamlets where services were held on alternate

Sunday afternoons and evenings in tiny little churches with pot-bellied stoves. In summer, Mother wore her white hat or her blue hat, always at an angle. People would come to hear the Shelby Family Quartet and on special occasions, like the Mayor's wedding, Mother and I would wear long black skirts.

I loved our family, my mother, my brother. But most of all, most especially, I loved, I adored, my completely wonderful father. He brought laughter into the house. He made everything happen. He delighted in our constant dinner parties with our best dishes and napkins in their silver napkin rings and the silver teapot and the little square sugar lumps in the silver sugar bowl. He was a happy man. I wanted to be like him.

CHAPTER FIVE

My Lord, how I loved him, child that I was. And how I do love him still. He is so alive, alive-o. You can see the vitality and the curiosity and the delight in his eyes. Last month we drove out to the lake and watched the sun descending gold and deep royal purple and red through the clouds. His face shone and his breath caught as he whispered, "Glorious. How glorious. Oh, if Meredith were still here. Do you see the glory, Mother? Are you in that glory, my dear?"

I held his arm and we walked slowly along the stones and the damp sand. Peace, I thought. Let there be this blessed peace forever. Let this be the final truth.

The seeds of peace were planted in my early childhood, in the storybooks and my teddy bears and Plasticine and crayons. The voices were soft. There was tenderness in the midst of our busy lives. Day by day, the laughter and the gentility were there.

The only area of tension that I can remember surrounded Father's constant travelling after he left the "radio ministry" and before the era of the Ontario Juniper Centre.

"I must be about the Lord's business," Father would say.

"There is that, and then there is the adventurer," Mother said with a turn of her head. Her voice, when she said this, had a bright edge to it which might have been admiration or envy, I didn't know which. I didn't think, at the time, that there was any judgement in the words.

Judgement had come, however, a few years earlier, from the brash new United Church minister, who was eaten up with envy and accused Father of "sheep stealing." Judge Grantham, the wealthiest and most prominent member in the United Church congregation, had defected to our camp. When he died, it was discovered that he had bequeathed his mansion and his spectacular thirty-acre property on the edge of town to Father's ministry. And thus began the breathtaking experiment in music from the heart of community, known as the Juniper Centre.

Father, the church wardens, plus Constance and James Hobbs—two well-known and innovative music therapists— and a few other high-ranking people from the church tramped across the rolling foothills, through the trees, along the stream. They dreamed dreams. Mother too was excited by the possibilities. One evening we had a campfire by a bend in the stream and Father said it was a perfect spot to create a beach and to build cabins. He talked of an auditorium, pointing to the area behind the stables, beside the swimming pool.

"A centre for Christian music. What do you think? James? Meredith?"

"Whatever Shelby says shall be," Mother quipped happily.

And so it was. The whirlwind toiled and rallied and preached, the women held bake sales and bazaars, the fund-raising committee applied to foundations for grants, the Hobbses organized concerts in which the Shelby family was always featured, and the money rolled in. The new auditorium was built beside the judge's stone mansion and connected to it by a glazed walkway. The rector's warden donated a grand piano. The local band led the townspeople in a parade to an all-day picnic which was held on the grounds. In the evening, my best friend, Janice, and I stood in the lobby of the auditorium, handing out song sheets. We both thought Constance and James Hobbs, tall and elegant, were the most beautiful couple we'd ever seen, Constance laughing and dancing. We followed them about, eager to be of use.

"Make a joyful noise, oh all ye saints," Father called out to the people. "If you can weep, if you can laugh, if you can shout, you can sing." And the singing that followed was directed to heaven.

It was an evening of improvisation and harmony, choral music, pieces by the band. Charlie and Father played a sparkling trumpet duet that brought the crowd roaring to its feet. The United Church minister, who was on the platform along with other dignitaries, made a moving personal and public confession.

"When I look out at this magnificent accomplishment, I am ashamed of the envy that found its way into my heart. Judge Grantham was right to entrust his land to this visionary in our midst."

Father, with tears in his eyes, walked up to the microphone and embraced his former rival. Mother, who was in the wings with Charlie and me, took a handkerchief out of her handbag and dabbed the corners of her eyes.

In the following months, the ordinary people of Juniper began to discover within themselves extraordinary qualities of musicality. "A community touched by grace," one commentator said. Father played recordings of "Songs of the People" on his radio programme and announced, "The Juniper Centre of healing through music has opened its doors."

One by one, from cities and from other towns, the curious, the tone-deaf, musicians, choir leaders and those in search of spiritual direction came to learn and stayed to serve, attracted by Father and by Constance and James Hobbs. More than one visitor commented, "This is a foretaste of heaven."

The theory was that the healing power of music was a two-way street. Lives overflowing with joy would find their most natural expression in communal song. Conversely, the activity of music would result in well-being. Song created health. Health created song. Instead of formal lessons, scales, arpeggios and drills, there was simply singing and singing and singing—playful songs, mournful songs, songs of praise, rounds, ballads, drones, chants. The centre was like a field of bubbles with music, the language of the heart, bursting out of windows and along corridors and in gatherings in the hills.

The catalogue and brochures advertised programmes that included after-school events, musical therapy sessions and weekend retreats. Within two years, a dormitory was added to meet an increasing demand for space for weekend festivals and conferences. Also within that time a kitchen band and five singers who had begun with rather ordinary voices formed a travelling troupe and toured the country.

One summer a journalist and photographer from a national magazine arrived. Charlie, puffed up with self-importance, was the official tour guide. Much of the article centred on an infant who had been found abandoned, and on the young waif of a mother, herself in need of mothering, who spent her days in therapy shouting and chanting and groaning. The photographer, who seemed to be in ten places at once, captured the large open play area populated by toddlers, volunteers and elderly people, two in wheelchairs, all playing drums and other rhythm-band instruments. There was also a shot of an agile grandmother who had climbed a rope ladder into an indoor "tree house" and was strumming a guitar while the infant rocked in a hammock beside her. The largest picture was of the round, recessed kitchen in the centre of the new dormitory with the cook who was quoted as saying she didn't have a musical bone in her body, but she knew about food.

It was almost half a year later that the story was published, but when it was out even the bishop called to congratulate Father. Uncle Jack brought over ten copies of the magazine.

✧ ✧ ✧

"You can't deny that hundreds of people have been brought back to life. He's been wonderful to people. Wonderful," I said to Charlie and Eleanor during one of our many arguments.

"He may be wonderful but 'flowers that fester smell far worse than weeds,'" Eleanor said, misquoting Shakespeare. "Both healing and harm from the same pair of hands. It makes me crazy thinking about it."

"And what about Mother?" Charlie added. "Think about what it was like for her."

Yes. Mother was always there. And she stayed there at the very heart of the torment. At the time, when I first found out, I blamed her. So, also, did she.

"It was my fault, my fault," she said. Mother, sweet Mother, was as sensitive as a snail's horns, and as unseeing. I now know that her cry was one of grief and madness.

CHAPTER SIX

Mother was lost that spring and I hadn't understood. The Hobbses were in charge of the Centre. Charlie was away at university. Father was also, as usual those days, away, away—travelling to India and other countries in the Far East, travelling to Europe, with his trumpet and slides. He was on lecture tours. When he returned, he stayed home less than a month, then he was off again, visiting the newest Juniper Centre in the North.

"Gypsies are gypsies," Mother said wistfully. "It's in his blood."

I'd see Mother going in and out of Charlie's room, straightening it out, puffing up his pillows. Once I caught her at his door saying, "You didn't turn off the light, Charlie."

"That was me, Mother," I said.

She looked startled. "Oh, how silly of me. Of course I know he's not here, dear. I do miss our menfolk. Don't you?"

"Yes," I said, but I was beginning to get used to it.

Another time I heard her say, "You're well and happy, aren't you, Charlie? That's all that matters, that's all."

After school one afternoon, Mother told me a letter had come. The North needed Father. "Meredith, I cannot tell you how small and undernourished some children here are," the letter said. "I am opening a public kitchen in the Centre." Father would be staying away for half a year.

"Six months! Oh Mother, how awful!"

Uncharacteristically, she clutched me tight. "We'll be all right, darling. We'll manage." Her voice broke as if she might cry but I dismissed the thought. Mother never cried.

I wrote letters to Charlie and Father. I told them about high school and how different it was from junior high and about events at the Juniper Centre. I told them I wished they were home. I asked Father to send pictures. I wrote to my grandmother in England as well—the last of my grandparents—telling her how much I missed Father.

Charlie rarely wrote back. One time his girlfriend, Eleanor, sent a copy of the university magazine with a picture of Charlie, tall and blond and handsome, under a flowering tree. The caption read, "Rare Juniper Songbird Serenades Our Spring." Mother laughed with delight.

Father sent postcards with cryptic notes. "The tundra is bursting with wildflowers." "Hope Paul and Terry [the visiting curate and deacon, who were in charge of the church in Father's absence] are managing."

My friend Janice and I spent most of our time after school and on weekends at the Centre. We'd get on our bikes and pedal out to run errands for the Hobbses or to take care of the small children or to listen to the band practising or simply to join in some group singing. There were always four or five people experimenting with instruments and new songs and harmonies. And there were always, of course, the boys we'd bump into. We'd rank them on the basis of intelligence and talent and looks. Janice and I didn't have much on our minds except boys and trying to look pretty and experimenting with orangeish lipstick and smearing gobs of Noxzema on our faces to fight our pimples, the deadliest enemies of all time. We'd talk about sex and where babies came from and what Janice's mother told her about the facts of life. My mother said sex was something the animals did.

In the summer, Granny Shelby gave me a ticket to England to visit her. It was the most exciting present I'd ever been given. "Wish I could go with you," Janice said. "Don't do anything I wouldn't do," we said in unison when we parted.

England was good for my skin. It must have been the climate and the water and the slippery goo from Granny Shelby's aloe plant. I returned in the middle of the summer holidays with pink cheeks and two jars of homemade aloe cream. Charlie and Mother were at the airport—Mother in her white summer hat, willowy and tall, and Charlie, even taller, beside her. As I walked towards them I thought how elegant they looked in contrast to the other people.

Mother smiled and held out her arms. Charlie squeezed my shoulder and said, "How's my high-flying kid sister?" Charlie was still Charlie although it was Christmas since I'd last seen him. The only difference was that his face looked cleaner now that he was shaving every day. He told me there was a surprise waiting at home and I played twenty questions all the way back and never guessed.

When I walked in and saw Father, he didn't get up. He didn't move at all. He was sitting on a cot in his study. He seemed thinner and shrunken and older. My body's first response was to jump up and rush to him, but the shock of seeing him so subdued stopped me.

"You're home!" I cried and stayed where I was.

Father's eyes met mine for the briefest moment. His smile was weak and forced. Then he looked to Mother as if asking permission to speak.

"Are you staying?" I asked, bewildered.

His eyes blinked rapidly.

"Yes, he is," Charlie said. Charlie was standing in the doorway, arms folded tightly across his chest, feet astride, nostrils flaring slightly the way they did when he had something difficult on his mind.

"Father's not well," Mother said softly. "We mustn't tire him, Millicent." She took my hand and tried to lead me out of the room. I resisted.

"You're ill?" I had never seen him so downtrodden, so not in charge.

Charlie cleared his throat and walked out to the hall. Mother put her arm around my shoulder. "No questions, Millicent. Not today." She was strangely intense as she pulled me forcefully from the room.

Before I went to sleep that first night home, she sat on the edge of my bed for a long time, holding my hand, patting my hand. "You're all right, darling, aren't you? You're all right." She told me that Father had come back suddenly. He'd sent a telegram, but he'd arrived before she'd received it. He was suffering from an enlarged heart. He'd been working too hard.

"You mean he had a heart attack? Why isn't he in the hospital?"

Mother glanced away and didn't reply.

Father was definitely and deeply changed. But he was still the person I loved more than anyone else on earth. I would go beyond world's end for him. I would do anything. But it seemed that in Father's eyes I had become a non-person.

"I wish I could think of important things to say to Father," I wrote in my diary. "Maybe then he'd talk to me."

The Juniper Centre had been a second home for all of us but now we no longer went there. In just one month my world had completely altered. It was as if I'd left an evergreen forest of brooks and wildflowers and happiness and while I was away some raging fire had destroyed it all. Day had become night. At home, I felt a steady unseen rain of ashes. Father hardly left the study.

"Is he going to get better, Mother? Will he be like he used to be?"

"We hope so."

Mother was, as always but more so now, showering her attentions on my big brother Charlie, my newly unbearable big brother Charlie. They were together all that summer, Mother and Charlie, Charlie and Mother, huddled with their whisperings, their sudden silences when I appeared. They had always been close. Now they were inseparable. Whatever Charlie said, whatever Mother said, the other would repeat like an echo.

"It isn't too much, Millicent, to expect you to clean up after yourself," Mother would say. And Charlie would say mockingly, "Yes, Millicent, you could clean up after yourself."

"Make sure there are no stains on the glasses."

"Or the plates."

"Or the plates. And do not raise your voice, young lady. You are a child of God."

"Remember that."

These bits of soot floated about in an atmosphere of nagging, of unpleasantness, of criticism.

Mealtimes were utterly cheerless. I would take Father's dinner on a tray to his study, then Mother and Charlie and I would eat in the kitchen as we had been so used to doing in Father's absences. Now, as always, the old alliances were being forged in petty domestic wars and kitchen chores. I was a sloppy, slap-happy Shelby. Charlie was a Hunter. Charlie belonged with Mother and Uncle Jack. Brusque Uncle Jack said this quite openly and Mother, rather than rebuking him, seemed pleased. "I do agree he takes after us, Jack. He's quite like you in some ways."

More than once I grew faint at the table. More than once I fled to my room. Charlie Jr. was obviously perfect. Millicent had to be perfected. Even the cherished realm of music suffered under the new regime. Where once I had played for the sheer joy of it, I was now required to practise the boring Hanon exercises, endless scales, chords, arpeggios. Technique became all-important and an end in itself. It was a complete reversal of the Juniper Centre model. If I complained, Mother would sit me down in the living room, open the Bible and make me read. Then she would begin her lectures on the sins of anger and impatience and disobedience.

It's only now that it occurs to me that Mother, with her unrelenting disapproval, may have been expressing to me what she could not express to Father. The praying and Bible reading and instructions in humility were interminable. She would not release me unless I apologized to Charlie and to herself. I would run weeping with rage to my room and stay until I felt somewhat restored. But when at last I reappeared, the lectures would begin again.

I was thoroughly wretched. I desperately needed Father, my old ally. I needed my friends. But inexplicably, Janice was now not welcome and I was not to go out.

"Why not, Mother?"

"Because we may be moving, Millicent. You'll need to sort out your things."

"Yes, sort out all your crazy things."

"Moving? Really? Where to?"

"We don't know yet. We're waiting for a letter."

"What letter? From whom?"

"You ask too many questions, Millicent."

"Millicent, stop asking so many questions."

I would not stop asking questions. "Why can't I see Janice? What's wrong with it? It's not fair." I hounded Charlie through the house. "What are you and Mother always whispering about?" I became the phantom of the hallways. I pretended to fall asleep on the couch hoping to eavesdrop. But the house was eerily quiet and for the first time in my life it was songless—no gathering around the piano, no choir members humming through the coming-and-going hallways.

Charlie, more bookish than he used to be, stayed in his room much of the time, reading, writing, sorting through papers, packing his books and trophies. Occasionally I'd hear him blasting a few notes on his trumpet and then he'd stop.

I was alarmed by the mysteriousness of it all. I tried to ask Father what it was about but he mumbled non-answers. "Go and help your mother, dear." He looked strangely injured and vacant, and at times he seemed cowed like a beaten dog, his eyes so oddly beseeching I could not bear it.

CHAPTER SEVEN

And then one afternoon, about a week before Charlie was to go back to university, the front doorbell rang as it seldom did those days. A delegation stood there—Mr. Grasser, the church warden, Mr. Stevenson, the rector's warden, the Hobbses from the Juniper Centre. Charlie, his head high and defiant, ushered them into the study where Father and Mother waited, their eyes glancing nervously at each other.

I tried to listen at the door. Charlie crept upstairs to his room, which was directly over the study. I tiptoed after him. He opened the damper of the heating grate and put his head flat against it. I wanted the corner of the grate but he waved me aside.

"Blasted lies," he hissed at one point.

"Let me listen."

"Get lost, Millicent."

The next day I was about to come into the kitchen and I heard Mother say, "But he *is* your father, Charlie. Please don't blame him. For my sake. If you love me—"

"But they were saying such heinous things."

"What *is* it about Father?" I asked coming into the room.

"Lurk, lurk," Charlie snarled. "Always lurking about."

"Father is feeling very, very badly," Mother said. "He has a bad heart and we mustn't make things harder for him. Now, no more questions."

The day before Charlie was to leave, I was helping him stack his boxes along his empty bookcases when the front doorbell rang again. Charlie and I leapt to the top of the stairs to see who had arrived this time.

The two church wardens, thin Mr. Grasser with his hat in his hands and kindly Mr. Stevenson, entered. Mother, looking flustered and patting her hair into place, led them to the study.

Once again, Charlie's head was flat against the heating grate. Once again, his hand impatiently waved me away. Then suddenly he scrambled to his feet, bumping into his desk, knocking over a stiff bouquet of yellow pencils in a marmalade jar. He ignored the loud crash. He brought down a box of books and tipped it over, pouncing upon the familiar blue Book of Common Prayer, the chunky version with the hymns at the back.

I followed him as he descended the stairs, riffling through the pages. He marched directly into the study, the book open in his hands.

"Sir." Charlie nodded to Mr. Stevenson, and said curtly to Mr. Grasser, "Sir, I apologize for interrupting. But I wanted to point out. . . ." He sounded pompous, and I could see the frown of annoyance on Mr. Grasser's face.

"It's all right, laddie," Mr. Stevenson said.

Charlie barely paused. "Article twenty-six," he said, pointing out the articles of religion at the back of the prayer-book section. He held the book in front of Mr. Grasser, who reluctantly took out his reading glasses.

"The ruling is here." Charlie's finger underlined the words as he read. "'Of the unworthiness of ministers which hinders *not* the effects of the Sacrament.'" He looked at Mr. Grasser and repeated triumphantly, "'. . . hinders *not*.' The sacraments are not affected, according to this, do you see?" Charlie's voice was getting louder and more aggressive as he read on. "'Although in the visible Church, the evil be ever mingled with the good, and sometimes the evil have chief authority in the Ministration of the Word and Sacraments, yet forasmuch as they do not the same in their own name, but in Christ's'—*but in Christ's*—'and do minister by his commission and authority, *we may use their ministry,* both in hearing the Word of God, and in receiving the sacraments. Neither is the effect of Christ's ordinance taken away. . . .'"

Father was wincing under Charlie's pontificating. Both the wardens had always liked our family, dropping in frequently for tea and cookies. They seemed to find the whole display pathetic.

Mr. Stevenson cleared his throat when Charlie was done and said quietly, "It's in the bishop's hands now, my boy. I have written a letter asking that our dear priest be permitted to stay on. We're discussing the matter right now. Your father has confessed. He has repented. And it's an exercise now in forgiveness that faces us all."

The people's warden frowned. "I don't know, Stevenson, that we can presume upon the mercies of the people. . . ."

I was halfway in the room, expecting at any moment to be asked to leave, embarrassed by Charlie's tone of voice, and wondering what all this had to do with Father's heart condition.

✧   ✧   ✧

Mother was the one who eventually told me about it. She didn't look at me. I had asked the questions one after the other until she gave the answers in one-word sentences. And then her mouth went small and tight and she sucked her lips in as if she would have taken the words back and swallowed them whole if she could. "It was my fault, my fault." She straightened herself, then drew back slightly at an angle, like a large tree leaning before it falls.

It was my Mother, I now know, who kept the world from imploding altogether—Mother, down through the years, her golden hair growing silvery, her porcelain skin becoming translucent, her clear blue eyes clouding. She, single-handed, with her unrelenting lifelong dignity, kept the stars from plummeting out of the sky.

I have found my diary entry for the day and it says I will never read the page again, I will never return to that day.

The house I built from that point on was made of wallpaper and paint. So much veneer. Mother helped. She did not once attempt to blow the walls down. We never ever talked of it again. Not once. And I now see that over the years, following that heart-numbing moment, my life's energies began to move differently. I no longer truly lived. I had begun to pretend my life. And I was never safe again. Everything I did was an effort to keep the roof from caving in. I feared any hint of inspection. I knew that the townsfolk, the neighbours, whoever might find out, would declare our home unfit. And henceforth and to this day I have lived in a world of fiction, so massively constructed that I have believed it at times to be safe.

It hasn't been hard to maintain the façade. For over four decades, we, the proud and proper Shelbys, have somehow conspired to keep the closet door tightly shut. When we enter our house of cards, we tiptoe about, not breathing, not whispering, making only the safest whitest sounds, like the happy sounds at Christmas—the jingling of bells, the singing of carols. Carol sweetly carol.

CHAPTER EIGHT

"I couldn't sleep, Father."

I have been staying awake for too many nights, listening to the termites nibbling at the paper walls. My brittle arms can no longer hold up the roof. I've been trying so hard to speak to Father. With each failed effort the weight of silence grows. Some days I feel I can hardly move at all—one foot in the slough of loathing, the other in the glue of love. I'm stuck. I'm wretched with knowing and not knowing.

It's strange how difficult it can be to manage a simple direct question. I sometimes come right up to the door. I put the key in the lock but I cannot turn it. The questions are stuck in my throat. I cannot say the words, even to myself. It's like being afraid of jumping into the water, being afraid of drowning and of choking and being dizzy and ill and never being able to take the words back again.

It must have been the same for Mother, that day after my conversation with Janice. It was months after Charlie had got in his parting shot on behalf of Father and had returned to university. I was in school again. We were, it seemed, not moving. At least, not right away.

After school on the first day back, Janice pounced on me. "What did you have? Measles? Mumps? Chicken pox?"

"What are you talking about? I wasn't sick."

"Oh. My mom said you were. I thought that's why you couldn't come out."

"No. I was packing. We're moving, I think. Maybe. I'm not sure."

"Is it really awful at your place?"

I frowned. How could Janice know anything? "What do you mean?"

"Oh, I don't know." She shrugged. "Mom says there are awful things going on at your place."

"Like what? What awful things?"

"She didn't say."

Then Sonia came up and whispered in Janice's ear and they went off together. "She's not your best friend any more," Sonia called over her shoulder.

"I don't care," I shouted back. I walked home as fast as I could. I hated them both.

Sonia and Janice were on their way to the Juniper Centre. I ached to go and see Constance Hobbs and have a groaning session with her. Janice and I used to go sometimes and groan our hearts out until we collapsed in giggles. But Mother said I had to come home immediately after school every single day and help her with chores—her ridiculous chores—cleaning out cupboards, washing an already clean floor.

She must have known I would hear about it eventually from someone at school, someone who would be unkind. Her anxiety must have been severe.

Janice told me one day that she knew Father was sick. "My mother says he's contagious. I'm not supposed to stand too close to you."

"What sickness does he have, Mother?" I asked. "It isn't just his heart, is it? Janice's mother said—"

"Janice's mother?"

"Said that Father has a sickness."

And Mother, who had her hands in the sink, turned away and said nothing. I persisted.

"Tell me what it is and I'll look it up in the library at school. I'll ask the science teacher. If you don't tell me, Mother, I'll go and ask Janice's mother."

Mother stopped then and her eyes were closed, as if she was praying. Then she took her hands covered with suds out of the sink and wiped them on her apron. She turned to face me but she wouldn't look in my eyes. She stared at the floor and her face became rigid, her mouth strangely twisted, tight and down. She uttered one word, flinging it from her as if it were a stinging insect.

"Sex."

"Sex?" I asked, completely nonplussed.

Her face of stone did not change as she kept her eyes averted.

"What do you mean—sex?"

She breathed in sharply and whispered one more word.

"Boys."

For a second her eyes grew large and there was deep shock in her face as if she could not believe what she had said.

I stared at her, waiting, trying to understand. Then I turned and walked away. I was bewildered. I went into the living room, where everything was just a bit tidier than it usually was, the big leather armchair where Father read the Bible, and the record player and the music albums against the wall, his trumpet on top of the upright piano, the long coffee table that had often been covered with his books and magazines. I went past the velvet drapes into the dining room and glanced into the crowded study-library-studio where Father lay on a cot covered in a quilt and a red and green afghan. He looked at me as if he knew that I knew. His face was tormented.

I couldn't think. I didn't really know what the two words together meant.

Sex.

Boys.

I tiptoed upstairs to my room and closed the door softly. I took my diary, my confidante, out of the desk drawer, unlocked it with the tiny key and opened to the blank page. I filled my Parker 51 pen that Charlie had given me with blue-black Waterman's ink. My handwriting was erratic, the tall letters spiked and craggy, the round letters cramped.

Dear Diary. Dearest, dearest Diary. Here is a page I will never again peruse. . . .

✧　✧　✧

There, Eleanor, I have said the words now. I have remembered what Mother told me and what Charlie said the following year—that Father was found out by two priests at the new northern Juniper Centre. I have written it all down in plain words here today in a way that I was unable to do then. I have lifted the lid of Pandora's box. Look at all the imps jumping with the tension of forty years' silence. They are mad with energy. Let us out! Let us out! Now that you have taken this tiny step, find out more and more. Learn, by the fly on the wall, what exactly he did. Find out, if you can, what happened to the boys. Exorcise the demon. Talk about it. Tell your friends. Declare out loud from the rooftops these things that were hidden.

Your father, say it Millicent, say it out loud—your father is a child molester. Your father is a pedophile or a pederast. Your father, your beloved father, whom you have loved more than life, is an utterly hypocritical degenerate.

In the days of his faithful ministry your dear father lusted after boys. "Boys," Mother said. They were children, then. He violated them. He silenced them. He lied to them. He betrayed them. In the secret of his days and nights, he stole the souls of the unsuspecting young and devoured them. Then boldly, in the clear light of the new day, with his white cleric's collar under his black priest's shirt, with his sign of holiness visible for all to see, he got in his car, on the train, on the plane and travelled on to other Juniper Centres, to small churches hidden in the hinterlands, to countries far away, preaching the Word of God, blowing his trumpet, as trusted servant, as priest, as visionary, as glutton, whose God was his belly. How often, Father? How many boys? How old were they?

❖   ❖   ❖

Across the landscape the clamorous shouting puts the birds to flight. "Away with him! Away with him!" The people versus

Barnabas Shelby. Here he lies, exposed to the skies, my father, my lamb, my Isaac. And over there beside him stands ancient Abraham at the impossible altar, frozen as in a painting, his eyes to heaven, his obedient pen raised in his foreverness of faith.

I can no more proclaim this truth than a stone can weep. Father is not Isaac and I am not Abraham at all but another biblical character, light-footed Jonah the coward, in flight from the task, leaping onto the ship bound for Tarshish—Jonah on the run, warning his shipmates he is hiding from God, hiding from the truth, terrified of he knows not what. He is crawling down to the belly of the boat. Oh, let him rather sleep. Let us return to the days when we proud Shelbys lived in the light, when we walked down the streets with our heads unbowed, when there was respect, sweet respect.

The density of the fog makes me dizzy. Everywhere around the ship, the nightmare is storming. In the middle of the tossing comes Eleanor, in the middle of the daily news is yet another story, in the middle of the uproar, so the Bible story goes, Jonah's shipmates come to wake him.

"What meanest thou, O sleeper? Arise, call upon thy God. . . ."

The facts give us no choice. Jonah himself knows it's the only way. For the sake of our shipmates, for the safety of society, in the name of truth we are thrown willy-nilly overboard where the large fish of mythology comes swimming along, swimming along to swallow us whole. The truth must be served, the truth must be endured, the truth must be told.

Here, now, we are crouching for three days and three nights in the belly of a cold fish. This is a place of waiting where there is no light on the topic at hand. Here in the world of the damned, by the dead desk, by the dead pen, there is only one word that can save us. Mercy. Mercy, dear God, in this cold and static place. Where Mercy dwells, there my heart's safety lies. Therefore do I seek her. Justice you can keep for a world that turns in time. For the sake of the saint that resides within him, let there yet be mercy for the criminal.

Did not Abraham bargain with God over Sodom and Gomorrah? "Wilt Thou really sweep away good and bad together?" Abraham dared to ask. "Far be it from Thee to do this—to kill good and bad together. Suppose there are fifty good men in the city? May I presume to speak to the Lord, dust and ashes that I am: suppose there are five short of the fifty— suppose thirty—suppose ten?" Suppose, dear God, that only ten per cent of Father is good?

Time is, as they say, running out. Time runs out of the mouth of the fish and the air in the belly grows thin. You have to get to the island before he dies. You have to obtain the sentence before it's too late.

As you sit begging in the dampness by the white bones of this large fish, you can hear a faint rustling sound, a bleating, a twig snapping. The ram, the sacrificial, ever-present ram, is stirring in the thicket of your mind and beckoning you to turn away from the harshness of a blood hungry sky.

"Blessed and timely ram, what is your name?"

"My name is Fiction. I am your fiction."

Thus is the name of the ram revealed by the Merciful One. Where the will to truth meets the will not to harm, a struggling fiction is found, trapped in the thicket and the brambles and the dense underbrush. By the sword of your pen, you are to slay your lifelong lies, your necessary deceptions, your subterfuge and inventions. You will grope among small white stones and through a house of bones, until you find your way to Mercy's throne.

And so, faint-heartedly, blindly, your body crawls across the floor, up to the desk, your hand crawls across the page, your white cane waves in the air, you tap your way a letter at a time in little blue luminous words on your portable computer, line by line onto the slippery screen, onto the blank paper walls.

CHAPTER NINE

There is a story of mercy that has come out of South America in recent years—a story of a good man and his torturer.

Torture. One hears that word screaming down through the ages. We are a species that does strange things.

The story is that the tables were turned and the tortured and his torturer exchanged places. The evil man was imprisoned. The good man he had tormented became his captor. Newly in power, the good and righteous man ordered the torturer to be brought forth. And here is the difference between depravity and glory. As the cowering prisoner was dragged terrified from his cell, his former victim embraced him, he kissed him, he freed him and he said these memorable words: "Thus do I take my revenge."

This is a story writ large in two men's lives. How much greater than the labour of the pen is the writing that is done on the parchment of our beings, on blood and bone and thought. While the foot still stays in the air, while the hand remains holding the knife, before the evil rides wildly over the streets, before it lurches over the hills and hangs itself from many trees, in the moment that goodness challenges wickedness, the telling word is written.

I do not recall the name of the merciful man. But I remember who told the story. It was Eleanor's much-travelled sister, Stephannie, who had returned from a trip to South America. As she spoke, her lips trembled, her eyes filled with tears. She had brought blessed news from the south. Good news. Mercy was still in the world.

Once upon a time, so another story goes, a dying man looked upon his killers and said, "Father forgive them, for they know not what they do." The man in South America was following a tradition.

In spite of these stories, it is not the God of the patriarchs I am seeking today. The God of my father has been made manifest in too much deception. I am looking instead upon the faces of women, in their strong or haunted eyes, in their rage and sorrow. It is not Abraham's but Sarah's deeper love that draws me. Her hand is that of stronger memory. Old, old Sarah carries the children still to come through the long red cry.

The power of the feminine, at some point around the eighth to tenth centuries, I'm told, overtook the masculine, and Kuan Yin, the male deity of mercy, became commonly known as Kuan Yin or Kannon, the Goddess. How or why this happened, I can only guess. Perhaps it was recognized that mercy visits us poor, naked beasts most often in the faces of our mothers, imperfect though they too are—our mothers who look upon us with pity when we fall, our mothers who themselves, like the waif at the Juniper Centre, are so often in need of mothering.

My mother, my elegant, dignified mother, was herself a motherless child. She was in an orphanage for a while. She did tell me that much. But I never discovered until after she died that she and Uncle Jack were illegitimate children. Father mentioned it in a casual comment as if it was something he thought I knew.

"Mother's parents were not married?" I repeated in surprise. I could hardly believe that she would have kept that truth from me. What other secrets, I wondered, were locked away in her lonely grave. Perhaps the stigma of her illegitimacy was what had sent her away from England.

I met her father, Grandfather Hunter, once when he visited us. I was four years old. Grandfather was a formidable man. He was able to catch sparrows with his bare hands. He cooked stews and baked and sewed and built furniture. He was able to find his way through the trees and over the hills without getting lost.

Mother was cool and polite towards her father. Uncle Jack was not. Grandfather wanted his offspring to return to England. We didn't go. Mother said Grandfather had a fierce temper. It's what had driven her mother away, she said.

Anger, for Mother, was the unpardonable sin. "You must say you are sorry, Millicent," she would say softly, bending over and taking my hands if I shouted in frustration. "You must not raise your voice."

Mother's childhood memories were all sad. She was three and Uncle Jack was two when they were left with strangers.

"You were babies!" I said. "How could your mother do that?"

"She had no choice," Mother said.

Mother's loneliness was profound. Once, while she was still at the orphanage, her mother came to visit and brought her a gift. Her father, enraged, made her return it.

Charlie and I always knew that Mother was not a person who could receive gifts—not our drawings from school, or the crafts we made at the Juniper Centre, not birthday cards, not Christmas presents. Everything we ever gave her was unused and wrapped and put away, quietly, without ceremony, without comment.

Eleanor was baffled by Mother but undeterred. She diligently brought the most thoughtful gifts and could not understand when Mother, who always thanked her formally, would then put the gift away. It was one of the things Mother did that I found embarrassing.

"I think your mother is quite strange, Charlie," Eleanor said once. "Quite aggressively strange."

About five Christmases ago, when Mother was very feeble, I wanted to use a beautiful casserole dish—one of Eleanor and Charlie's many gifts hidden away in one of her closets.

She was surprisingly coherent, sitting up in her bed. "I keep it wrapped that way, Millicent—you may wonder why—but it's because love is there," she said. "Love is in that present." Until that moment, I had not understood that gifts were too precious to touch. They were icons. If I had known, I would have given her the world. I would have given her my heart.

There were so many things I never understood about Mother. In the year of Father's fall, she was a ship hit by lightning. But no one told me. The water was pouring in. She had to find a way to stay afloat. She clawed at her daughter. She clung to her son.

My estrangement from her lasted her entire lifetime. I did not like her—the dead weight of her unhappiness. I do not like the dead weight of my own. Claws, Mother. I still need to claw my way out of the ocean depths. How many of us are down here in the silent waters, curled up into ourselves with our untellable tales? I can barely scrape my way along the ocean floor and over the small bodies strewn about like undecipherable hieroglyphics.

What are the names, Father? What was killed in each one?

CHAPTER TEN

In the end, Mother and Father and I stayed in Juniper. The letter we had awaited, the letter from the bishop that would tell us our fate, came about a month after Charlie left. Father took the envelope into his study, where he had been lying on his cot for weeks, staring at the ceiling, and closed the door. Minutes later, he called for Mother. When they emerged, Mother put her arm around me and said, "Father is going to see the bishop, Millicent."

"What for?"

"To see what God wants us to do."

That was all she said. Father drove to Calgary the following week. When he came back, I stood beside Mother as she took his hat from him and hung it on the coat tree in the entrance. She held her thin hands to her throat as she waited for him to speak. He did not look at her. He smiled wanly at me. Then Mother and Father disappeared into the study and the door was closed again.

I learned later that day that the bishop, in his wisdom, had decided that Father was to go on a retreat for a month to the mountains. After that, Father saw the bishop once more and we were permitted to remain at Juniper.

"We are in a time of testing," Mother said. "In such times, we are to cling to God. The more punishing life is, the more we must cling."

Mother ascended to a life of prayer. I would come home from school to find her at the kitchen table, the Bible open and passages underlined in red beside her. More often she was in church, kneeling at the railing, hands across her chest, eyes lifted to the empty gold cross in the centre of the altar. She read devotional books. She became a devotee of the Christian mystic Sadhu Sundar Singh.

As soon as Father was back from his month of solitude and prayer, Sunday services resumed, but the people, except for loyal Mr. Stevenson, no longer came. Most of the congregation joined the United Church. The Anglican stalwarts drove thirty miles to the Anglican church at Cuthberton. Where once our church had been bouncing with a choir, Sunday school and a constant stream of people, there were now times when only Mother and I were in the pews, walking up to the dark oak railing, kneeling to receive the wafer and the wine. Father, attired in his black and white robes, would stand at the lectern or in the pulpit against the dark walls beneath the stained-glass window, reading the prayers and lessons, giving the sermon, announcing the hymns, his voice ringing out over the absent choir, the absent congregation. Mother played the organ, singing as loudly as she could. I chanted the responses. Together, we three were imposing the order of sound, a sound

order, over our abandoned lives. The Lord's Prayer. The
Magnificat. The Nicene Creed.

"'The peace of the Lord be always with you.'"

"'And with thy spirit.'"

Every Sunday began with early morning holy communion
at eight, then morning prayer at ten-thirty, evensong at seven.
My knees were sore from too much kneeling.

Mrs. Stevenson, the wife of the rector's warden, attended
services a few times with her husband, but during Father's
sermons she would take out her Bible and ostentatiously read
to herself, her lips moving silently. She had stopped her ears.

One Sunday Mr. Stevenson brought Mrs. Parker, an elderly
widow who couldn't keep driving to Cuthberton. Father wept
when he saw her. "God bless you, Mavis," he said, taking her
arthritic hands in his.

Father gradually came back to himself. He read Norman
Vincent Peale. He dwelt on the positive. Occasionally we
received visitors from out of town who knew nothing about
the scandal and his full-bodied laughter was there again, warm
as sunshine. But we never went back to the Juniper Centre. The
"community touched by grace" no longer included us.

Father and Mother found their new ministry elsewhere,
among the sick and the old and the destitute. They visited "the
fatherless and widows in their affliction." Mother was practical
in her compassion. She took food. She swept floors. Father
went to court with criminals and stood by their families. He
wrote letters on their behalf. Our home became a hostel for the
homeless and travellers, and people were coming and going in
the halls once more.

"It is well, it is well with my soul," Father and Mother sang.

I believed them. But Charlie did not. Charlie, whose defence of Father had been so forthright and vocal that terrible summer, turned from him the following year. He walked away from Juniper, from us and from the church. He switched his entire allegiance to Eleanor, truthful, courageous Eleanor, who was three years older and a decade more mature than he was. If Eleanor had not been such a strong believer in family ties, we might have lost Charlie altogether.

They were married in a small brick church in Eleanor's home parish of St. Chad's. All of Eleanor's Edmonton relatives came out in force—her parents, an aunt, her two brothers and their wives and children. Her younger sister, Stephannie, came all the way back from Sweden to be the bridesmaid. Throughout the ceremony, Stephannie's mischievous little toddler, Martin, was prancing about making a nuisance of himself. Father caught him as he ran past down the aisle and carried him outside. Stephannie glanced back gratefully.

Mother's tight smile throughout the wedding was a mask. Charlie, the light of her life, was now taking all his cues from Eleanor.

It may have been around this time that Father began to create his own publicity. As the applause he craved no longer rained down upon him, he began his own campaign of confetti, paper praises, self-congratulations. Boasting increasingly dominated his conversations. He wrote articles trumpeting his past glories and successes which I had to take down to the local paper, the *Juniper Sentinel*. I dropped them off hurriedly at the counter, but Mrs. Paulie, the publisher's wife, was almost always there and I thought she looked at me with pity.

The items were usually printed and Father would read them and seem satisfied.

"Oh, people are so good to me. So good to me," he'd chuckle to any and all who would listen. He'd invite strangers to dinner and prattle on endlessly. He may have been egocentric before, but I had never noticed.

In Charlie's presence, however, Father became a submissive, ghostly man. Even the most innocent thing he might say was greeted by Charlie with sarcasm and scorn. One Christmas we were at Charlie and Eleanor's place and Eleanor's father offered him a glass of wine.

"Oh, that would be wasted on me, I'm afraid," he said. "I don't drink. I've never imbibed alcohol, you know. Never smoked. Not once."

"Oh sure," Charlie scoffed. "You're so pure, Father."

Eleanor's father coughed with embarrassment. When Father tried to change the subject and talk about one of his trips, Charlie cut him short again. "The travels of the prodigal father," he jeered.

Father offered no defence. He was always on Charlie's side, even when it was against himself.

"Charlie is right. I am a weak man."

I saw Father as King David, crying out after his traitorous son. "Oh Absalom, my son, my son."

He was always giving Charlie gifts, large and generous gifts beyond anything he ever gave Mother or me, including the down payment for a car and his tuition at university. He offered to publish Charlie's thesis on sects and cults in Western Canada. One time when Father was still in recovery from an appendectomy he went to Charlie—King David on his knees, crawling to his favourite child, the beautiful one, his hard-hearted son. I wept for Father. I railed against my brother. I accused him of not being able to forgive.

"Forgiveness is everything," I said. "It's what we're here for."

"If you want to be biblical about that," Charlie replied in his churchy voice, "it's the powerful who are enjoined to forgive the weak. It's not the other way around. The rich forgive the poor. The poor have debts. The king's subjects don't forgive the king. It's not your place to forgive Father."

"Well I don't care what you say. I do forgive him."

"That's not forgiveness. You're his child. It's bondage."

"No it isn't. It's love."

"Love without truth," Eleanor shot back, "is a cheap sentiment."

"But what I feel isn't *cheap!*" I cried. "And anyway, Father isn't the king. He's the weak one. You're the king, Charlie. Can't you see that? You're stronger."

As Father became more and more servile to Charlie, I worked harder. I bought cards full of extravagant praises. "Happy Birthday to the world's most wonderful father." I pleaded with Charlie to be more kind. I reasoned. I begged. "Think about what the Juniper Centre means. All that music. All that fun. Think about how many kids and whole families have been brought alive."

Never once did Father say a negative word to or about his son. When I criticized Charlie, Father would say, quietly, "He has your mother's soul, dear," or "Charlie is the light of my life." I didn't stop to wonder what that made me. I just wanted the happiness back.

In spite of my best efforts, I watched Father deteriorate. His bragging betrayed the storyteller within who told him opposite truths. He wanted to drown out Charlie's voice. So did I.

Charlie and Eleanor increasingly absented themselves from our family gatherings and rarely drove down to Juniper. When on occasion they did come, the tension was unrelieved— Charlie scorning Father, Mother fawning over Charlie, Eleanor enduring it all.

Mother was also deteriorating. At times she was quite odd. During one of their visits, Charlie and Eleanor came down with Stephannie and her rambunctious little Martin. Stephannie, who was getting a divorce, wanted to be a free spirit and travel all over the world. It seemed she was trying to bring up her son to be at home anywhere.

"He's quite comfortable sleeping on buses or planes. He's quite well adjusted," she said, smiling and kissing his nose. "Isn't he, my little Marchinsky?"

I had my doubts. He was the most demanding child I'd ever seen, the only four-year-old I knew who constantly asked to be carried.

We had barely sat down for dinner—Martin was picking out all the carrots from the vegetable soup—when Mother suddenly said, "Let them go home now, Father. Isn't it time they returned home? We should let them go, dear." And she began clearing the table, her mouth wrinkled shut.

Eleanor flushed red. Stephannie looked at Mother curiously.

"Please sit down, Mother," I said.

Charlie grimaced and kept eating. Charlie and I had been arguing about Father, who was planning to go off again on another trip—back to India and the Far East, the Philippines, Indonesia. Father was under the bishop's orders to travel with

Mother but, bishop's orders or no bishop's orders, Father intended to travel alone. I urged him to do so. I knew that was what he wanted. I was the only one to support him.

✧   ✧   ✧

"Slay the fiction," my Goddess has said.

Once upon a time my mother was the perfect clergy-wife. I believe what broke her spirit in the end, more than anything Father did, was Charlie's rejection. Perhaps her two main fictions of a devoted son and her husband, "a good man," could no longer be maintained.

Once upon a time I believed that Father, in his travels, was serving God. That was what he said he had to do. And since I did not have in my possession God's Book of Days, I could not know what terrible harm was being done by him in the North or in the Far East, or how many boys there were or what he did to them.

We walk through life having to slay so many of our cherished beliefs. Too often our truths turn out to be lies, the evidence does not stand, facts no longer support our stories, and we find ourselves adrift, without guidance, without comfort and searching for stars in a starless night.

The Goddess herself may be just another fiction, arising out of dream and desperation. Or she may be beyond fiction. I cannot say. But I shall not slay the hope that lies within me that I may find the power of mercy and the pathway to the abundant life. Along the way I am to sweep aside the temporary structures where I have lived for too long. My old house of lies is to perish, that a new and better house may be built.

CHAPTER ELEVEN

The new and better house of my adolescence was a house
made of clouds. Reading back in my diaries, I can trace my
frantic efforts to keep from crashing on the rocks below as
the Shelbys fell from grace. I had been flung from a place of
high regard, from a right and wrong, clearly marked world,
and was floundering in outer space. I was scraping the skies.
I had few tools with which to construct a shelter of reality in
that sudden coldness. Out of the ether and the airwaves I
manufactured my secret house of solace. I lit my fictive light
and warmed my heart. Blessed fantasy, blessed fiction, blessed
denial that enabled me to survive.

I was barely fifteen when the lightning and earthquake first
struck and the crack in my foundation walls appeared. I was
sickly that year. I finally understood the snickering. I missed
weeks of school. I developed the habit of walking rapidly,
books clutched to my chest, eyes on the ground. I did poorly
in my grades. I was then and still am today terrified of the

aftershock that could bring our entire house down.

"Don't talk about it," a voice within me still says. "It's too dangerous." If the hatred, if the atavistic rage that is out there in the world erupts, if the hounds are set loose, Father will not survive. Neither will I. As I watch the news these days, I shudder at the media spectacle as one old man after another is dragged from the safety of his anonymity to face the stoning. No one is more loathed today, inside or outside of prison, than the pedophile.

Once upon a time I discovered a beam of moondust and followed its pale light to a make-believe world so compelling that it took me years to emerge from its spell.

It began with the utmost subtlety—with the sounds of coughing or throat clearing, with the slide of a desk or chair or shoes on the classroom floor, with the colours of shirts and blouses, with a piece of paper crumpled into a ball and tossed into a wastebasket. Every tiny bit of evidence became the stuff of secret communication.

He was real. His name was Stewart Barton. He was the smartest student in the grade ten class. He sat three rows across and two seats in front of me. He wasn't handsome but he was brilliant. He wore glasses and his small round ears stuck out of the sides of his head like little toadstools. From the back I knew when he was embarrassed because his ears would grow red.

My mind was fixed on Stewart. He would walk into the classroom and *voilà!*, he would be wearing a blue shirt perfectly matching my blue blouse. The next day his shirt would be plaid. I would have the same colours more or less in my skirt. It was uncanny. In English class, the teacher would read a poem out loud. At crucial moments he'd cough, his head would turn slightly in my direction. He was signalling to me. I didn't dare to catch his eyes.

The fact that Stewart was dating Janice caused me grief. Nevertheless, in the mulberry bush of my mind I was going round and round gathering nuts in May, morsels of nourishment. He dated her because she used to be my best friend, did she not, and it was a way of being close to me, for after all, was I not a talented Shelby? And then one warm evening, as I was playing the piano and singing some English folk songs with the windows wide open to the night breezes, I saw lights from a vehicle outside flashing on and off. I kept singing.

Early one morning just as the sun was rising
I heard a maiden singing in the valley below. . . .

There was a sharp whistle. I stopped and glanced out. Beside the big willow tree in front of the house was a pickup truck. Stewart had a pickup truck. I got up from the piano, left the living room and went upstairs to the darkness of Charlie's room. From behind the safety of the curtains I peered out. A lanky figure was leaning against the side of the truck. Stewart? It looked like him.

Another night, when I was in my room upstairs, I heard the truck again—this time in the back alley. There were voices. The light from a flashlight shone in a wide arc and touched the neighbour's chimney and then my window. It had to be Stewart.

Every few days my diary had entries about his many foot-scraping messages, or the code he tapped on his desk top or the way he deliberately tried to get me jealous by putting his arm around Janice. Whatever he did, he was signalling to me. On the days that our colours didn't match, it was because he was annoyed with me. We were linked by a mutual and secret obsession.

Then, in the spring, the fiction developed into a deeper implausibility. The moonbeams found a way through the walls.

One weekend afternoon I was listening to a symphony concert on the radio. My fiercely romantic heart was transported out of Juniper into a distant glade, into a walk along a seashore with Stewart, into fairyland. As I dreamed the hour away, a ghostly girl in my ghostly world, I began to note that sounds of static surrounded a particularly melancholy concerto—the same piece that we had been listening to in our music class. At first it was only a suspicion, but the following night it happened again. As the radio announcer talked, his words were punctuated by static. The signals were unmistakably specific. "And so all you listeners out in radio land *(static)*, send me your letters. There's nothing better than being in direct communication *(static static)*." I was convinced. Stewart was now talking to me through the radio, letting me know which music most moved him and connected us. I was in direct receipt of his thoughts and his often humorous comments. He delighted me. He enraged me. He moved me. He was my source of happiness. Incredibly, I would sometimes hear tiny buzzing sounds in my electric heating pad and these too were originated by Stewart.

In the next stage of my growing unreality, I suspected and then I knew that Stewart, my genius, had designed and created a device by which he could see into my room. How else could

I explain the way the radio static punctuated the sentences at the very moment I was writing them in my diary?

"Are you there now Stewart?" *(Crackle crackle.)* "You are!"

It happened repeatedly at precise points of significant comments, or whenever I wrote his name, for example. When I realized that he had the power to look into my room, other pieces of the puzzle locked into place. I understood how he was able to wear the same colours as I did, day after day. I became embarrassed to undress. I took to kneeling behind the bed where I thought he could not see.

All the way through high school, I kept the secret of Stewart's great powers to myself. I made no overtures to him in any open or public way. There were times when Janice and I were friends again and I wondered if Stewart could hear what we were saying.

"Do you believe in ESP?" I asked her one time.

She shrugged. "Do you?"

"Yes. But I can't tell you with who. It would break it if I told you."

After graduation, Stewart went to one university, I went to another. But late at night the radio static would continue, and on certain weekend nights I'd recognize the sound of his vehicle and I'd rush to the dormitory window, or I'd hear the signal of a car horn and wonder if Stewart was still faithfully prowling the streets.

"Are you out there this minute, Stewart?" I asked my diary. "Do you remember our happy days in Juniper? Do you miss me as much as I miss you?"

Years and years later, in a moment of easy intimacy and growing doubt, I spoke with Eleanor about "a genius I used to know."

"Oh Millicent, he couldn't have had a machine like that," she said. "To build such a thing? No."

"It wasn't possible?"

"No."

That simple word and the chuckle that accompanied it were the first major assault on my fantasy. Gradually over the months and years, as I graduated to other forms of moondust, Stewart faded from my mind, and my secret place of solace vanished like the house of smoke and mirrors that it was.

❖   ❖   ❖

My adolescent fiction was slain without a psychiatrist, without pills and without labelling. On the surface I've managed to appear calm, but inwardly I'm as tentative and unstable as a ping-pong ball. I still fly through the air, scraping the skies for evidence of love.

CHAPTER TWELVE

I have made lunch for Father. The usual. Soup and a sandwich. Tomato soup today, a bit thin, cheese sandwich.

"The soup is rather weak, I'm afraid," I say apologetically.

"It's fine, Millie dear. Perfectly fine." Father is so polite. He has always been so polite.

I look at his tranquil face. There is not an angry line anywhere—no hardness around a tight mouth, no frown of impatience—a few deep smile lines around his round dark eyes, a few lines of curiosity on his high forehead. It's the beatific peaceful face of a child or a saint. Small wonder that people smile at him so readily and greet him with reverence. "Isn't he radiant?" one woman in church whispered. "What a joy your father is."

How can any of us know anything about one another except through the evidence taken in by our eyes and ears, except by what we sense in their presence? "He's a genuine innocent," his doctor said recently. Father, in his old age, continues to have a child's enthusiasm for life, still trusting, still welcoming strangers into the house, and still delighting in having afternoon tea with the old silver tea set as he and Mother used to do every day.

In the past decade, as Mother weakened, Father kept up the habit of inviting neighbours in for afternoon tea. Throughout her growing senility, he attended upon her day and night, dressing her, combing her hair, bathing and feeding her, cooking and shopping.

"Meredith, my sweet, shall we put on your lovely pearls today?"

He was her willing and happy slave. People visited them like pilgrims to a shrine. This is the simple truth, Eleanor. I can swear on my mother's grave that Father was devoted to her, that he cared for her as tenderly as a mother cares for her baby, that with patience and forbearance he watched over her, indulging her throughout her late-night wanderings, her mind-impaired repetitive speech, her confusion, her fits of incomprehensible laughter. He called her "my queen" as he took her hand and walked with her through the garden, examining the roses.

"Can you remember the day Charlie was born? Can you remember what day your birthday is, dearest?"

She was so deaf he'd cup his hands to her ear. She refused to wear a hearing aid. "Barnabas is a good man," she would chant suddenly in the middle of conversations or during grace.

There were days when Mother was so confused she didn't know where she was—in England, or Alaska, or still in our old house in Juniper. She never quite got used to any of the people in Ragland, this picturesque lakeside resort in B.C. that Father chose for their retirement years. Ragland was a good choice. The winters here are snowy but not too severe.

Father, the once well-known host of "Shelby Selects" and founder of the Juniper Centres, was eagerly welcomed by the priest and parishioners of St. John's Church in Ragland. But Mother, increasingly deaf and senile, was unable to keep up.

After years of driving back and forth between Edmonton and Ragland, I finally moved down so that I could keep an eye on Mother when Father went away on his many trips. My apartment was two blocks away. But a little over a year ago, as her condition worsened, I moved in to help Father.

Occasionally, I would suggest that she be placed in a nursing home, especially after she became incontinent, but he would not hear of it.

"Mother belongs at home," he said firmly.

I arranged for the homecare worker to come an extra day a week to cope with the huge pile of laundry. The house smelled disgusting—urine and mouse droppings and old food. I bought stacks of Attends, the diapers of old age, and potpourri and deodorizers and new slippers. I called in the carpet cleaners. I had the leaky washing machine fixed. I even brought home a kitten from the SPCA—a black and white female. Boots was a good mouser and quite amusing. She had a way of wanting to lick people's noses with her rough tongue.

Father was grateful for every little thing I did. "You're so considerate, dear. Thank you so much," he'd say. "What would we do without you?"

I told Charlie that Father was a wonderful nurse. Charlie said Father only took care of Mother because of the praise he received from guests. I disagreed. Anyone could see it was love.

His face was wreathed in smiles and he walked through the days like a bubble, lightly. In his old age he was living an enchanted life. "These are the happiest days of my life," he said.

Charlie's voice on the phone whenever I praised Father was tight and tired, stretched out like old elastic ready to snap. The admiration he'd once had for Father had so withered away that it was as if nothing, no heroics of any kind, could revive it now.

Charlie has never been one to want to talk about personal matters. I would try sometimes to get his feelings on our family's fall from grace, but he would only sigh and shake his head. "You can't break away from it, can you?" he said once, when I was up for a visit. He was trying to read, sunk deep in his armchair, while Eleanor and I talked, half watching the evening news.

"You mean *you* can?"

"I've got a life to live. I've got Eleanor, thank God. And Eleanor's family."

"My family?" Eleanor laughed. "You mean my crazy sister Stephannie and her weird son? My family's warped and woolly too. Whose isn't?"

"Your parents are great," Charlie said.

"That's true. How the two of you have survived your mother and father, I cannot imagine."

"Mother isn't so bad," Charlie said.

"You don't think so? I think she's crackers," Eleanor said. "But it's your father who's—"

"It was Mother's fault," I interrupted. "If she hadn't been so frigid. . . ."

"Don't be ridiculous," Eleanor said. "Your father hasn't got a conscience. She's not the cause of that. She *is* icy, but who wouldn't be around *him?* Don't you see the way he's always trying to use people, always trying to see what he can get away with? It's just a wonder that no one's tried to strangle him."

Charlie, who was still trying to read, turned the volume up on the TV and asked if we wouldn't mind talking somewhere else. And then Eleanor asked him, as if only my presence, the blaring news and the book could cushion the impact of the question: "Charlie, did your father ever—did it ever happen to you?"

"What?"

"I mean. . . . That. You know what I mean."

"Oh. That." His eyes had the slightly faraway look that Mother so often had when she was perplexed and sad. He shrugged. "No, not me." He hunkered down into his book.

Eleanor wouldn't accept that simple answer. "How do you know, Charlie? He's so corrupt anything's possible. Maybe you were too little to remember."

"Well, who knows," Charlie said, and turned the page rather aggressively.

Eleanor has always had a singularly uniform and bleak view of Father. But I believe the truth about him to be brighter, stranger, more terrible and complex than we can know. What I want is for all the truths about Father to be brought forth. I want his pastoral labour to be known, I want his furtive deeds to be dragged from the dark dungeons. I want the sick who were comforted as well as those who were harmed to bring their stories forth.

"The truth is, he's got a cog missing," Charlie said. "The truth is, he can't die because he isn't at peace."

"That's not the only truth, Charlie."

Here in the town of Ragland, people still flock to him. A young couple dropped in today, deeply distressed, grieving the death of their only child. He placed his hands on each of their bowed heads. "My children," he whispered, his voice filled with tenderness, "take heart. There is One who knows us and loves us beyond all comprehension. We can go to Him who holds Becky forever safe."

In his private life he is faithful in his devotions. Every morning around five, Father reads the Bible and says his prayers. He has a prayer notebook with the names of people to whom he is intimately connected by letters and phone calls. Every day, he faithfully prays for each one, and sometimes he becomes aware of someone in special need. Later a letter will arrive telling him what he learned while in prayer. Over the years, the corners of the notebook's pages have grown thin as dragonfly wings.

"Why," I asked him one time, "do you pray for so many people every morning?"

"Because," he replied, "the spirit moves in the lives of the people as I pray."

Miracle is part of his daily life. Last week, for example, he felt the urge to call Godfrey Adams, an old friend in Ontario. I overheard bits of an intimate conversation, Father listening, responding. "I'm glad to hear you say that, Godfrey." They shared a few moments, gliding through the air together on the wings of prayer. That very afternoon, Father received a letter from Mrs. Adams asking Father to call, saying her husband was suffering from severe depression and had not been able to talk to anyone for months.

"I had no idea," Father said, marvelling. "He spoke perfectly clearly to me." He shook his head in wonder as he read the letter.

And a month ago, on the way to testify at a court hearing for a young single mother, Father fell on the sidewalk and injured his back. His face was white with pain, but he would not be dissuaded from helping.

"You are so very kind, Father Shelby," the young woman said as she held his arm and tears welled up in her eyes. "So very good and kind." The judge too seemed impressed.

These daily realities cannot be adequately described. But neither can they be slain. When Father is gone, the effects of his wrongdoing will continue, but his loving deeds too will remain. Whatever the two words meant—*sex, boys*—I still cannot imagine that Father ever intended harm.

I go in and out the windows of my mind, in and out, back and forth. How can a man so good be so bad? How can a man so bad be so good? He is loved, he is despised, he is Jekyll and Hyde. The puzzle spins from dark to light, light to dark, as the earth spins, as the sun spins, as my mind spins and reels and burns a black hole in the palms of my praying hands.

✧   ✧   ✧

Dear Goddess, could it be that we humans are simply wild beasts on the dreaded island of Dr. Moreau, children of the knife, being sliced and cauterized and sawn asunder by a Creator hungry for drama? I am flying over the madness on your magic carpet and look down upon the poor maimed animals, their forelegs clawing the air as they hobble and hop to their clearings and caves. There they gather at dusk to chant their creed. "We shall walk upright. We shall not kill. This is the law. Are we not men?"

In spring the waters come rushing, surging onward, shaking the ground. The creatures fear it. They watch it from the safety of banks and bridges. When it breaks the acceptable bounds, when it threatens to flood their towns and pleasant villages, they gather their forces. "We shall contain the rage. We shall build our walls."

But look over here, over the towers and rooftops, over houses and churches, where a creature sits brooding. Look at the rising lust in its loins, rising like the sap in the tree. An uncontrollable passion seizes its limbs. A sharp intake of breath and the energy surges through its body. This is the moment when right gives way to wrong, to untamed passion, to body hunger, to the madness and thrill of the uncivilized appetite, the moment when remorse, obligation and all humane urges are lost in the chase.

Who is that furtive half-creature, late at night now, lurking in the foliage by the forbidden glen? Down on all fours lopes the lion-man, King Barnabas. In the darkness his eyes are luminous as the moon. His tawny hair bounces in the night breeze as he leaps upon his prey. As high as the sky is the small animal cry.

Good Lord deliver us! Good Lord deliver us!

In the daylight, the monarch is back in his palace, sitting on his throne, surrounded by his court. He is the wise king reigning over his pain-racked kingdom. Each day he leads his writhing subjects, the maimed and crippled half-human forms, as they whimper and scream their praises to their maker, Dr. Moreau.

Kyrie eleison
Lord in your mercy

And then one early not-yet-dawn, the king's daughter rises from her dreams into the teal blue sky and the blossoming perfume of the summer. She peers out of the palace windows to the marketplace where the monkey-men pedlars have not yet arrived to set up their wares. Down the palace corridor she hears the pad, pad of the king's royal feet and she springs to the door to greet him.

In the instant that he bounds around the corner, the king sees his child. He shakes his heavy mane as he stands upright and roars, "Go back to your slumber, my child. The sun has not yet banished the night."

"Father!" she cries, her eyes wide. "Father, what is that cut on your brow? That blood on your mane!"

In the twitch of a lion's tail, he turns from her and leaps from her sight.

The king's daughter trembles in terror. She has caught the whiff of animal blood in the palace, she has seen the stains on her father's face. She knows the law of the Lord. All transgressors are sent to the dreaded chambers where God wields his knife and the screams never cease.

She stands in the long vaulted hallway as the first rays of the sun touch the golden skylights, flooding the palace. But the king's daughter no longer sees the glory. Before her spreads a dark crimson glow.

She waits outside the king's chambers. She wants to warn the king in case God should appear. She runs to the edge of the forbidden glade. She wants to warn the small animals in case the king should appear. Back and forth she runs till the sinews in her legs grow frayed from the exertion. Everywhere she goes now, under sunlight or birdsong, the king's daughter feels treachery. She sees God in the marketplace questioning his creatures. "Tell me," booms the Almighty, "who is it among you who runs on all fours? Who goes to the kill? Who has broken the law?"

In her mind, she hears her father's plea as he stands before his Maker, his proud head hanging low. "It was beyond my control, My Liege."

It is God who will decide if King Barnabas will be destroyed or reformed.

"Ah, if I could sing a beautiful song about his greatness and bravery and wisdom, perhaps the Master would not slay him, perhaps the souls of the small animals would forgive him," she says to herself, and every day she sits at her table by her window, composing a ballad. But the words fail her and her heart grows heavy. She knows she is powerless to change or redeem him. However much she tries, she cannot erase his crimes.

One day the king says to her, "Why are you sad, my daughter? If you have done no wrong yourself, then you have no need to carry a burden."

It seems strange to her that he, who has done so much wrong, should be aware of the weight of burdens. Why is he not crushed by his? Is he too a victim of himself? Is he, as victimizer, carrying a far greater load than she can ever know?

Oh if the forest creatures could understand that he is as much a victim as his own victims—that he is helpless against himself, weak and blind—if they could see the good within him, they might love him again. But she can hear their rage. "If he is blind to our suffering, let him suffer until he knows ours."

"Will my suffering suffice?" wonders the princess. "If I am tossed into the flames, will this be an act of atonement? Will their pain be eased if mine is increased?"

"Not at all," whispers the wind. "It is not for you to usurp for yourself the power that belongs to Love alone. Mortal flesh cannot claim the role of the immortal."

"Then what must I do?" asks the princess.

As she ponders her questions, to which no answers come, a great melancholy descends upon her. She looks in the mirror through her eyes, which are her father's eyes, and she no longer recognizes herself. Is she still the good king's good daughter? Is she the evil king's evil daughter? She is a child of iniquity, flesh of corrupt flesh. How could she, tainted as she surely must be, know good from evil?

She is desperate for answers. As the child of a lion-man, she knows that to capture the truth she must stalk it downwind, move in obliquely, trap the truth with the sound of twigs snapping before it knows it's being pursued.

"Father, tell me about goodness. Tell me about evil."

"About such things, my child, one need not ask."

"And are you not good?"

"I am a lion."

"With my own eyes, Father, I have seen the red stream trickling along the forest floor. I have seen the blood."

The king turns his face from her and beckons to his courtiers. "Sing," he commands, and at once the trumpets sound, choristers appear and shout together, "The king is virtuous. Long live the king."

The king's daughter knows then that her father is lost. "Ah, dear Father," she weeps as she watches him smiling, nodding, waving to his subjects.

She runs crying to the small animals in the far dense woods. "My friends, what must be done to repay his crime? Tell me what I must do." But the small animals flee at her approach. They hide in the highest branches and in the deepest burrows and all is still. The leaves do not rustle. And more silent than all the silence is the stream that washes away the scent of blood. She goes to sit beside it.

"Tell me, tell me, is there anything I can do?"

Hour after hour goes by as the weight of her wretchedness overcomes her. What she wants above all is permission to love her father again as she once did. She wants this so intensely that the lines between good and evil are increasingly blurred.

Then one evening at dusk she becomes aware of a strange buzzing sound. As she listens, she begins to understand words, then sentences, whispers, suggestions, and because she is utterly wretched, she wants to believe what she hears.

"It is not the king who has failed," says the tiny voice, "but the world that is wrong. It is not the king who has failed, but the understanding that is wrong."

She looks about to see where the words are coming from and notices a gnat flying by her ear. It is one of a swarm of gnats from around the spoor of a large wild animal.

She captures the whispering gnat in her hand and takes it back to the palace, where she puts it in a bottle and wraps it in layers of mouldy comforters. She places it in a trunk in the palace storeroom. She does not dare to ask herself if the gnat might be right. But secretly she goes to the dark room to listen.

"If you want to talk about perversion," giggles the strangely soothing tiny, tiny gnat, "what about Leda and the swan? What about frustrated spinsters who twiddle their pets? Think about the South Sea island where mature women initiate boys. If you think there's anything abnormal about the king, just enter the secret fantasies of anyone on the street. People demonize in others what they cannot accept in themselves. Buzz buzz buzz."

"Tell me more, little gnat," she says urgently as her thoughts become less and less clear. The gnat weaves tales from other ages and places with other rules, other customs, other laughably quaint moralities, until her mind reels with confusion. "You've heard about how Egyptian nobility once had sex with their young?" More and more boldly, like a king entering his castle, the gnat enters the edifice of her thoughts.

"You know that the king is good," says the gnat one afternoon. "More than all others in the kingdom, you know this. Others may well declare that he is a cunning pretender, but you alone in all the world see the tenderness in his gaze, see the kindness, as he smiles upon the world with his large happy eyes."

"Yes," weeps the princess. "About his love there is no doubt."

Armed with these thoughts, one sleepless night the king's daughter decides to go to the Master to ask for his mercy. Carrying the gnat in its bottle, she sets out on her journey. She goes first to the jails, then to the gatherings of the Ku Klux Klan, and the Nazi Party, and the altars where children are sacrificed, and into the forest glade where psychopathic killers stalk their prey.

"Come forth, all you who are most feared and despised, all sadists and rapists and murderers, all you who harbour in your bodies raging unquenchable fires. Come forth and be visible.

Make your unknown stories known. Bring your love of Wagner, your bowls of milk for your cats, your tender lullabies, your prize roses—bring your full humanity into the clear light of day where you can be greeted as the familiars that you are. Bring with you just one person who has loved you, for when you are loved you are blessed with that presence forever." She goes next to the fields, and along the train tracks where people watch as the trains roll on to the gas ovens. "Come all you who stand and stare, all you who click off the late-night news and the sight of children starving and dying. Bring your scholars and psychiatrists and armies of gnats and let us go, one and all, blind and helpless creatures that we are. Let us seek an audience with our Maker, the One who has made us and who loves us as we are."

Thousands upon millions of maimed, stumbling creatures join the squealing, snorting, braying parade. At its head, let loose from its bottle, flies the now quite strident gnat.

❖   ❖   ❖

"There isn't a single undusted corner in my mind," Eleanor said that September night last year, her voice rising, "not a single spot where I entertain a speck of doubt about child abuse. Not a jot."

"But what if it's mainly a cultural problem?" I asked. "Didn't we burn witches at the stake not so long ago? How do we know we're not doing the equivalent thing today?"

I had ordered all the gnats in the island to come and sit on the telephone lines, even though I knew they were no match for Eleanor. She could kill them all with her spray can of truth. I'd seen her do it many times. She'd walk into a room thick with petty gossip or misinformation of some sort and—poof!—truth would happen.

"You sound just like Martin," Eleanor sighed.

"Who?"

"Don't you remember my sister's son?"

"Oh yes. Stephannie's little boy. I haven't seen him in decades. How is he?"

"Not so little now."

"I used to wonder how he'd turn out. Is he still a handful?"

"Worse. Much worse. He's staying with us—temporarily, we hope," she groaned. "I have to tell myself he *is* my sister's son. He has no success in forming lasting relationships at all. Stephannie was shortchanged in the family, I think. I could tell you tons of stories about her and you'd understand where Martin's coming from.

"I got a letter from her the other day from India," she continued, "saying we've got things backwards over here and North America is, of all the continents, the poorest of the poor, because there's no sense of community here any more. I believe her. People like your father do the things they do because they're in hell, they're isolated. If we could really connect with him, he wouldn't want to go back to hell. The best model I've heard of for people like your father is the Native healing circle. The perpetrator is there, and the parents and kids and the victims and all their families and neighbours, and they each get to talk. We should all do that. I've got an idea, Millicent. If you can't talk with Father, I should come down to Ragland. I think—yes—I should bring Martin along. He's part of our circle, and we should all talk. Martin has a lot to say."

"Oh please. I don't think Father could stand it."

"You're wrong, Millicent. What is unbearable is the not talking."

"It's—it's just too unkind," I said. "He's so old. Let him have his peace."

"Peace!" Eleanor's aggressive voice sounded anything but peaceful. "Oh yes! Peace! I'm all for it. How on earth can we have peace if we don't deal with this?"

CHAPTER THIRTEEN

"Well, well." Father opened his arms wide to the stocky bearded man standing in the doorway. Martin, with a crooked grin on his face, said, "Hi there, Pops." Mother pulled herself up from the couch with her cane and clutched Father's arm anxiously. "Who is this, Father?" she asked tremulously. "Doesn't he know you are a minister of the church?"

Mother was fairly lucid that autumn afternoon last year, but Martin was a complete stranger to her. I too would not have recognized him. He had a dark, raggedy beard and wore a black leather jacket with silvery chains. Gone was the perky little boy in short pants calling us Auntie Elly and Auntie Mills.

Mother stiffened and tried to pull back when Eleanor hugged her. Father offered Eleanor a chair. She barely looked at him, and sat on the edge of the seat, her whole body leaning away from him, her legs tightly together.

Tea was an awkward affair. When it was finished I said, "Let me show you the town." Eleanor looked a little relieved as she

got up. I wondered if her resolve to question Father had weakened when she'd seen how impossibly aloof Mother was. No
matter how hard Eleanor tried to be friendly and intimate over
the years, Mother kept the wall of formality firmly in place
between them.

It was a warm day. We strolled down to the park, Martin's
longer stride carrying him ahead so that he had to slow down
every so often till we caught up. He turned to frown at Eleanor
when he heard her say, "Your father's bizarre predilections."

"Sensibilities change," he said. "Thomas Aquinas thought
masturbation was worse than rape, you'll be interested to know.
I bet we'll have adult–child sex legitimized in the next—"

"Never," Eleanor said icily. "Not in a million years. If we do,
it won't be a world I'll recognize. Whatever's left of the sacred
will be gone. Sexual abuse—"

"There you go," Martin interrupted, slapping his forehead.
"That word again. Abuse! Please. Use the right term. Call it
sexual pleasuring, will you? When I was a kid I *loved* sex. I'd say
to myself, 'If it moves, fondle it.' What's the matter with everyone today? What happened to 'make love not war'? The body is
sensual. Right from birth. It's built in. Have you ever watched
little kids? They love their genitals. I played with myself all the
time. That's the problem. People forget. You know, a few years
ago nurses used to rub the winkles of newborns and that was
the most natural thing in the world. Even babies masturbate.
So if an adult does it with them or to them, why the hell is that
shocking? Look, even Kinsey thought it was okay for a kid
unless, of course, you told him it was"—Martin threw his
hands up in mock dismay—"hey—oh my God kid, you've
got—yeuch—a penis. Oh bad bad."

We had reached the flower beds at the cenotaph in the middle of the park. Eleanor and I sat down on a bench, but Martin continued to pace in front of us, one thumb hooked in his belt loop. Some children were swinging in the play area nearby.

"I could get arrested just for going over and talking to those kids."

"Oh come on, Martin," Eleanor said impatiently.

"It's crazy. What's the message? Anyone who touches you is a devil? What are kids supposed to feel about what they feel? They'd be a lot better off if we'd just enjoy their luscious little bodies. What's so wrong with kissing, snuggling, even copulating if they want to?"

"You make me shudder," Eleanor said.

I couldn't tell if he was being serious or deliberately outrageous.

"*I* make *you* shudder," Martin scoffed. "It's people like you two goody-goods. You go around damning anyone who's really alive—adulterers, bisexuals, pedophiles—anyone who dares to be different. It's envy, isn't it? Admit it. Your lives are so sanitized you don't know what's natural. And you're jealous. You're jealous of freedom. All through history it's people like you. You stoned the witches. Or people like me or your old man. Drown us. Burn us at the stake. You think you have the right. Now that's abuse of power with a capital A."

"The truth of the matter—" Eleanor began.

"The truth of the matter," Martin cut in, "is that 'the passion for boys and for women derives from one and the same love.' Know who said that? Plutarch."

"I know the ancient Greece argument," Eleanor said. "Ancient Greeks were barbaric. What the powerful wanted, the powerful got. Slaves. Boys for sex. And *that's* abuse of power. And let me tell you, Martin, if you want to know what's natural. Your love map is so distorted you don't know what healthy sex is."

"How dare you!" Martin flared. "What makes you the arbiter of health? Why should I be judged by the likes of you? Why should the highly sexed, the sexually gifted, be judged by the dimly sexed? I know, I know, you can't help it. You were born sexually retarded. People are born the way they are. There's no virtue in that. It's genetic. Child-lovers are born child-lovers. You've heard of Klinefelter's syndrome?"

Eleanor's eyes were large and piercing with anger, but her voice was measured. "Molesters are not born molesters, Martin. Even if they're traumatized when they're very very young. Even if they're imprinted. There's choice. That's what makes us human. Not all molested kids become molesters. And if it *were* natural, it would still be wrong. It might be natural to steal and kill. But we don't do it. There's no justification for pedophiles. None. None. There isn't a spot in the moral universe where pedophiles can stand."

I sighed. "But if you knew Father the way I do. . . . There's a part of me—there's such a big part of me that wants to see all this the way Martin . . . well, not exactly the way Martin does, but. . . ."

"Oh, Millicent, why should you twist yourself into knots? You know the abuse of children is an utter abomination—you know it in every bone in your body. It's deeply deeply damaging. Permanently damaging. It's like cracking open the shell of an egg before it's ready to hatch. It cripples people for their entire lives."

"Not me," Martin said.

Eleanor ignored him. "The structure of the imagination gets destroyed. We've learned about this. People with multiple personalities, prostitutes, drug addicts, suicides—this is the fallout of abuse."

"And so it's open season on pedophiles today," I said. "They're the single most abhorred people around."

"Because they destroy the lives of children. They kill the future. It's that simple."

"But if you love someone more than your own life, you go anywhere with them—even beyond yourself, beyond the edges of the known moral universe. That's what love does, doesn't it? It goes to the edges and leans out to whoever is lost. Like Jesus. Or even Gamaliel. . . ."

"Who?" Martin wanted to know.

"Gamaliel. A man who had the decency to doubt. And he said, 'Wait. Let's not be too hasty in condemning Christians. Who knows? Maybe God's on their side.' Maybe Gamaliel would say, 'Hold on folks. Why are we in this frenzy about sex and kids?'"

Eleanor was aghast. "You can't compare pedophiles to the early Christians. Really, Millicent!"

"Well, I know, but. . . ." I looked up at the sky and the yellowing leaves overhead. Eleanor wasn't willing to entertain any doubt at all, but what could any mere mortal know with unwavering certainty?

Eleanor turned to Martin. "Why don't you tell her what you told me?"

"What for?"

"Because"—Eleanor lifted her hands, palms up in a gesture encouraging speech—"she has a right to know." The look that passed between them as Martin shook his head told me enough.

"You're trying to tell me," I said carefully, "that Father—that he—that he's the one who. . . ."

"Yes," Eleanor said. "He did molest Martin, and not only that. . . . There's something else Martin should tell you."

Martin looked away. "He can tell her himself," he said and turned on his heel. Eleanor hesitated, sighed, then stood up wearily and followed him.

"Tell me what?" I called after them.

She phoned me later from a motel. "The real harm to Martin was what it did to his mind. Can't you hear him making a case for cannibalism?"

"He must wear you out. What is it you wanted him to tell me?"

Eleanor breathed in sharply. "Millicent, I've wondered about this. But I know I. . . . If it were me. . . ." She was silent for a moment and I could hear Martin's muffled voice in the background. Then she was back speaking to me, repeating my name, and I could hear her breathing unevenly as if she was trying hard to speak. Once or twice she took a deep gasping breath and I thought she was about to begin, but she didn't.

Next day she called me in the early afternoon from Edmonton, as I was in the shower. "When you don't know something," she was saying, "it's like carrying around balls of sticky fuzz. Questions stick to the palms of your hands. But truth is firm. Truth makes all the gooey edges become solid and you can put the matter down and get on with other things. I have to know the truth about. . . ."

"Is this about Charlie? Are you still thinking that. . .?"

"No. It's about something Martin told me. Martin told me. . . . Are you sitting down? Sit down, Millie, because . . . because I. . . ."

"What is it, Eleanor? What are you trying to say?"

"Millie. Oh Millicent. . . ."

As she spoke, sobbing and choking, I slid to the floor. I sat there and sat there and then I started dialling the long fourteen-digit number beginning 0 1 1 then 4 4 for England.

PART TWO

CHAPTER FOURTEEN

In the faraway island of Dr. Moreau, the years went by and the years went by and the king's daughter spent her time by the silent stream with the countless gnats that twirled and swirled and spiralled about. She drifted more and more into sleep, into a world of dream and shadow where her father was once again upright, unblemished, lordly and good. But beyond the silent stream was another world of courtiers and minstrels, a forest dripping with gossip and whisperings, full of wild and peaceable beasts. Into such a world, the king's daughter brought forth a child, a comely, bright-eyed baby boy.

The morning that he was born, the king's daughter lay in a pool of exhaustion and light. With her hair still damp from the exertion, she held his small, downy head and body in the cups of her hands. Her fingertips kissed his pink, wrinkled face, his little hands and toes. She cradled her baby to her breast and wept with utter joy. This small new being she loved with the ferocity of all the royal blood to which she was heir. She loved him more than the entire world, more than life.

Daily she nursed her infant son and sang him lullabies. He cooed, then crawled, then babbled and danced about as he played with the small animals who came to the stream to drink. Lovely and laughing and full of song was he, and as vulnerable as the tiny wildflowers on the damp forest floor.

These were her days of happiness. The sunlight was gentle, the breezes warm. But into her pastorale, stealthy as a thief, crept mist and cloud, came the sound of muffled weeping and wailing. Now once again and more than ever, a heavy gloom engulfed her, and the daughter of the part-lion king knew no peace.

At night, she hid her child beneath petals and leaves. She guarded him by day, her eyes alert. She shouted at shadows. She was fearful of she knew not what. Every morning dawned, blue sky and blossom, and everywhere there was danger.

Over the years the boy gradually matured surrounded by his mother's watchfulness, her fierce and tender love. He grew strong and straight as the trees in the forest where he wandered. His mind was pure and clear as the water from a fountain that cascaded and tumbled in the village square. Each morning the sun continued to rise, and each day the boy continued to be safe.

She couldn't quite pinpoint the moment, unlike her son, who in later years remembered exactly what happened—such is the power of our memories about such matters. She recalled later that he had changed rather suddenly from being a somewhat audacious and growingly rambunctious youth to a docile, curiously cautious and somewhat cooperative boy. She remembered being pleasantly surprised.

Many many years later, when the king's daughter did finally learn the truth, it all became more than she could bear.

✧   ✧   ✧

It is more than I can bear, my Goddess. It has become more than I can bear.

I asked Jeffrey last year and he told me he thought I knew. He thought I knew. I was asleep in a house of lies, dreaming that I was awake and attentive, that I was a good and careful mother.

✧   ✧   ✧

"Perhaps he was not hurt," whispered the gnat. "Perhaps. Perhaps."

"Amen. Oh may it be so," prayed the king's daughter. "Let us say he was not hurt."

The madness converged in her mind as a wild and heavy grief, a black rain that descended over everything. It covered the entire island, the marketplace and the palace where the king sat on his throne.

With her hands stretched ahead of her, the king's daughter began to walk through the rolling mists of space.

✧   ✧   ✧

Look little tongue, little dart, little poison arrow, little tattler of tales, go quickly and pray as you fly that your words may be true—to kill what must be killed, to free what cries to be free.

What is it that weights your small heart shape? It's the salt, the too-much weeping as I walk through the day-after-day, carrying the ocean, wearing the ocean, bearing it. Bearing it.

✧   ✧   ✧

The cup, when it can no longer contain the rain, overflows. The heart, when it can no longer bear the sadness, breaks. Life, when it sufficiently wearies, ends. I have begun to imagine the end again. Like a crack in the window, the thought spreads across my mind.

✧   ✧   ✧

Jeffrey. My dark-haired, brown-eyed, perfect baby boy. My son. Eleanor's darling. Our child. Jeffrey.

✧   ✧   ✧

My baby was born at seven fifty-two on a Sunday morning in the Vancouver General Hospital—Sunday's child, full of grace. The labour lasted twenty-two hours. He was pulled from me by forceps wielded by an inexperienced young intern. It must have been the strangest anaesthetic that was used because I felt no urge to push; yet, after the baby was pulled out, the sewing up of the tear was excruciating.

Boy Shelby. Six pounds seven ounces. Mother: Millicent Shelby. Age: nineteen. Address: Rachel House.

There were six of us unwed mothers among the dozen others in the large ward, in beds side by side and across from each other. One sixteen-year-old was, like me, from Rachel House, a godforsaken home for fallen women. Once a month we had been driven down in a windowless van for checkups at the Vancouver General Hospital outpatients' clinic. We were all guinea pigs. During one session, the young intern had my feet up in stirrups as he paraded one classmate after another to gawk at my private parts. The times were not kind to young women in our circumstances.

We who found ourselves at Rachel House all had our stories, true stories, false stories, wretched stories. We were all to give our babies away. We were counselled to do so.

"If you really love them, you will want them to be in loving homes with fathers. When the children grow up they'll be grateful to you. Think of Hannah offering up her son Samuel when she brought him to the temple. Girls, you are Hannah's daughters."

As the baby's kicking grew in vigour and as the time neared for the delivery, my nightmares increased. I lay with my bulging body stretched out beneath society's guillotine. My fate had been decreed. I was to be severed in half. The sylvan cord between myself and my child was to be torched and our love and longing for each other crushed. I did not weep. I wrote to Eleanor and Charlie that, God or no God, right or wrong, I couldn't go through with the plan.

Rachel House had been Charlie's idea. "At least, there, you'll know you aren't the only one in your predicament," he said, slightly caustically. That was true. Eleanor thought I should go as well. Vancouver was far enough away. I didn't know anyone there. She and Charlie were going to be my baby's parents. They would adopt him immediately and take him back to

Edmonton. I would go later and no one would know. I could be the visiting aunt. It sounded like a good idea at the time. But in the end, my arms won the battle. In no way did I give the baby up. I told the young doctor that I was keeping my child and I would nurse him. The other unwed mothers in the ward looked on with envy as I held my tiny bundle to my engorged and blue-veined breasts. The teenager in the bed beside me said her parents would disown her if she kept her baby.

The whole saga began the summer after my second year at university. He was from England, a short, intense, older man with receding hair, the author of a book on medieval music. He had been hired to direct the popular and highly successful Juniper camp in Ontario. I was in charge of the younger children.

"You have quite a name to live up to, Miss Shelby. A remarkable man, your father," Dr. Jonathan Steele said when we were introduced. His grey eyes searched mine as he removed his dark-rimmed glasses.

There were a thousand small choices along the way. He was experienced and I wasn't, but I have never absolved myself of responsibility. When he tapped on my window at night I could have stayed in the cabin. We walked along the beach. He put his arm around my waist. I did not pull back. I should have asked the appropriate questions.

I first noticed his attentions before the meals, when I would lead the children in the singing of the grace. I caught him beaming in my direction across the hall of tables, and as the rounds ended he would wink and smile. At the evening campfires, he sat on the log beside me. One night, after the children had trooped off for hot chocolate, he whispered, "I could listen to you all night, Camper Songbird. I love your voice. Would you come and sing just for me?"

"I'd be happy to, Skipper Steele."

I knew and didn't know, as he took my hand and led me into his secluded cabin, that I wasn't the only one. He lit a candle and brought out a bottle of wine. He asked me if I was afraid.

"I don't know," I mumbled awkwardly. I moved back slightly as his hand inched across the sheepskin throw on his couch.

He told me he had a favourite sentimental old song. "'In the Gloaming. . . .' Do you know it?"

"Mmm. Sort of. . . ."

"Would you sing it for an old fool?"

I laughed and hummed the tune.

"Melissa," he whispered as the song concluded.

"Millicent," I corrected him.

He asked me if I knew any arias. I was embarrassed as I grinned and shrugged, then let my voice climb an arpeggio to a high, tiny trill. I felt ridiculous and giggled.

His eyes were wide and intense, almost as if he were afraid. He moved towards me so gradually it was as if he weren't moving at all. Then suddenly, as I stopped singing and his lips touched the tip of my nose, he drew back. He stood up abruptly and said he was terribly sorry, it was all a mistake and I should leave. "Now. Right now. You must."

"But. . . ." I backed up against the couch, both hands over my heaving chest. "Have I done something wrong?"

"No, no. Not at all. You have done nothing wrong, child. But leave, quickly, quickly."

All that week he avoided me. Instead of sitting beside me at the campfire and joining in the skits and stories and songs, he stood in the darkness near the water's edge, far from the glow of the fire.

I became obsessed. The more he turned from me, the more I sought him. One night I walked back and forth along the path between our cabins, aching to see him. He told me later that he'd been watching me from behind the wash house, and he'd known then there was no way out for us.

The first time was late at night, in the thickness of the forest a long way upstream, by the waterfall. All the way down the garden path and up the trail, I made my tiny decisions not to resist. He caressed my neck and his fingers pulled softly, playfully at my ears.

I did not know who Dr. Jonathan Steele was. I did and I did not trust him. He was the camp director. He was the one who every morning told the morality tales and directed our minds and hearts to purity, to nature, to love, to God.

Once his hands touched my abdomen I was lost. At that point, it was beyond my control. My hands gripped the sides of the rough tree bark as he thrust against me. Out of the push-pull confusion of desire and dread, I wept and cried out. He wrenched me from the tree. Half clothed and struggling, I was brought down to the earth, to pine cones and needles that scratched my limbs. I lay bruised and bleeding under the camp's captain and the waterfall's cool spray.

After that, nothing mattered. I was doomed. He was a married man. I was indeed not the only one. But the great cloud of unreality that clothed my life told me he would love me and only me. He would leave his wife. And night after night I returned to his arms, to his cabin, to the woods, to the wash house, to the beach, to the struggle and the pine trees overhead and the distant distant stars, farther away than anyone could imagine.

I had written him three letters before I knew for certain that I was pregnant. In my panic that day, I walked out of the doctor's office, went to the bus station and waited three hours for the bus that would take me to Charlie and Eleanor.

CHAPTER FIFTEEN

Merciful Goddess, it is a lifetime later and I am still waiting at the station, trapped in distress, curled into myself like the half-burnt red ribbon I discovered in the fireplace this morning. Tonight I offer you my wretchedness. I bring you the busy streets along which I stumble and the corners where I fall, the vomit spewing forth, the passersby walking in quick and kindly anonymity, the gentle fireman at the fire station to which I drag myself, who takes my pulse and asks if he should call for an ambulance, and the garbage pail with cigarette butts that he brings and the green bile I spit as I shiver and weep. And in the midst of it, I want Father. I want his warm hand on my head and his eyes to heaven, praying. . . .

✧   ✧   ✧

Goosey, goosey gander,
Whither shall I wander?
Upstairs and downstairs
And in my lady's chambers.
There I met an old man
Who would not say his prayers,
I took him by the left leg. . . .

✧   ✧   ✧

I watched him saying prayers with a young couple today. He comforted them. He comforted me when I was weak. I am still weak. And in my weakness and bondage, my body rejects its undigestible knowledge. I take him by the left leg. I throw him down the stairs. I fling myself into the gutter beside him. . . .

✧   ✧   ✧

Like a crack in the window-pane, didn't I say, the thought spreads. . . .

✧   ✧   ✧

Gentle people of the jury, I, Millicent Shelby, the daughter of the Reverend Dr. Charles Barnabas and Meredith Shelby, I, the unwed mother of the beautiful young man Jeffrey Charles, yes, Charles—Jeffrey Charles Shelby—I, my father's daughter, am sick with a sickness I cannot name, and I want my father dead, I want him dead.

I am told that unless I enter my grief and rage, I will in no way walk through the gates of the beautiful city. You see my body shouting its revulsion on the sidewalks and pavements of Ragland, on the corner of Main and Second, on a noisy Tuesday-cheap-movie-night, in the middle of cars and trucks and the people promenading to and fro. You see me as I lurch about and stumble with my grey leather boots covered in what I cannot deny and you hear the young cowboy hooting because he thinks I am drunk. "Can't hold it down, eh?" he laughs, and rolls on past as a taxi arrives and I am driven back here, to the house of lies.

I sit in the house of lies, I am looking into the abyss. From out of the darkness, as I peer over the edge, I hear the one impossible command. I am to declare the truth.

The truth is, I cannot endure the truth.

One word at a time, Millicent. One step, one step. As we walk, we are the way. We are born as tiny specks of hope to glow and fade, forming ribbons of light that wend their way through this tortured world. Each choice makes the next one easier. With each deception, each moment of courage, we define who we are, for good or for ill. Are we not ourselves the way the truth and the life?

✧   ✧   ✧

I am taking time out now to run a bath and wash my hair. I will soak in the hot water and the perfume and foamy suds and bubbles and listen to some harp duets. And after that I will try to sleep.

One does grow weary.

❖   ❖   ❖

It is past midnight, and I am weak and restless and lonely as I wander out the kitchen door into the garden and down the empty back lane looking for you—on past the cenotaph, past the lakeside hotels with their all-night restaurants and up Main Street again. Merciful Spirit, where are you?

Near the end of Third Avenue, by the corner to the back alley, I see a gaunt, stooped, dark-skinned man staggering, hitting the wall of the bank as he coughs and spits out an incoherent sound. "Garrarara!" He is unwashed. His face is streaked with dirt. His puffy hand grasps air as he reels and rocks back and forth. I walk past quickly, but when I turn my head I see him fall. I look again and recognize a fellow traveller curled up in a familiar gutter, groaning, retching. This man is a drunkard. I too am drunk, reeling with conflict, hand extended for help, waiting at the side of the road for the Good Samaritan to come by.

Here in the dark-sewer night, you send fragments of old Bible tales, morality lessons written in the wind. You send a wounded messenger whose word, growling through his crumpled body, speaks of misery. Here in this world of mirrors we are less than a step away from a psychiatric ward, from a prison cell, from being stoned by the crowd.

As I bend forward to peer at the fallen man, I catch a sharp whiff of alcohol mingled with the odour of his unwashed body. The back of his jacket is torn. His face is pocked and blotchy and his nose has a dirty Band-Aid over the bridge.

The ragged man of Ragland struggles to his feet and, waving his arms about, he stumbles forward and back, forward and back, like the waves on the shore. He lurches towards me. I flush with embarrassment and anxiety as I retreat.

This is the place to which you have brought me today. This is your world and your wilderness and there is no *Gloria in Excelsis Deo* to greet the shepherdless sheep bleating on the hillside here. The darkness glows with red-hot coals of shame and disgust and lifelong pretence, and we, your blind-eyed children all, call out to you. Do you not see us in our red and yellow and orange flaming robes as we dance screaming in our excesses and our so-great follies? We are lost and in distress, waiting for the Good Samaritan, waiting for Godot. What are we to do?

We are to seek mercy. Steadfastly, within every hell to which we are heir, we are to seek mercy. From within the reality of overwhelming shadow, we are not to make a fiction of the reality of light. With our eyes wide open we are to rush headlong, impetuously, desperately, through the terrible light of our fears and our truths, glancing neither to the left nor to the right, till at last we come to the Mercy seat.

And so, because I am like this broken man who can barely stand, and because there is nothing more that I can do, and because I have no other avenue of hope or escape, and because my old fictions tonight lie dead around me, I am reaching out to Mercy with my entire being. You have brought me to this scorched-earth place, to the heart of the flame. Here in the heat and ash is where you are. And though tonight a square moon should rise in the staring sky, though the headlines should blare the unthinkable news, you will remain here beside me in this safe place of ashes where the difficult labour of health must begin.

And nothing, nothing is required of me except to be with you as I face my truth. This is my truth. I am the child of a child molester who molested my child, my fatherless child.

CHAPTER SIXTEEN

I asked Jeffrey and he said he thought I knew.

He thought I knew.

"How old were you, darling?"

"Twelve, I think. Yeah. Twelve."

"And what did he do?"

"Oh, it was nothing, Mom."

"He touched you?"

"Yeah."

"Often?"

"Just once. It was nothing." Did I detect irritation in his voice? "It's like what a doctor does. He pinched."

"He pinched your penis?"

"Yeah."

"They put people in jail for doing that, Jeffrey."

"Yes, but I think that's wrong. He's just a. . . ."

"Just a what?"

"A funny old guy. That's all I thought."

"But he's your grandad."

Jeffrey wanted to dismiss the whole thing. He was uncomfortable. "It's no big deal, Mom. He's not violent or anything like that."

Maybe this was denial. Maybe it was truth. Or part denial, part truth. More than anything in my life I needed Jeffrey to be well. The big question in my mind had to do with harm. At the very least, that act of invasion could not have helped him. But I had no way of knowing the nature and the extent of the damage. The scar might be so deep that it could threaten his stability to try to dig it out. I thought of asking him to talk with a psychiatrist but I knew he wouldn't. I found myself saying lightly, "As long as you're okay, darling, that's all that matters to me"—hearing, in my own voice, my mother speaking: "You're well and happy, aren't you, Charlie? That's all that matters. That's all."

Over the following weeks I found I could not keep thinking about it. I simply could not. My heart and mind did not have the resilience or the strength to take the fact of the matter in and stare it down. I was altogether weary. I buried myself in caring for my mother—until Eleanor would call and bring it back to the surface.

"Are you really sure he's telling you everything?" she asked.

"I do *not* want you to call him, Eleanor." I was emphatic. "He's been invaded enough. I don't want you to bulldoze his walls down in the name of truth or anything else. If he's living in a little mental shantytown, if he's fragile and tenuous about all this, I don't want you to unsettle him. I don't want a homeless child."

"Do you realize we're breaking the law by not turning Father in?"

"For God's sake, Eleanor, we're family!" I didn't ask her what she would do if she were the daughter. Being who she is, she might very well have reported her own father. She is the only person who insists on talking about all this. Charlie certainly doesn't. If Charlie had married a different kind of person, someone less truth-obsessed, it's quite likely I would have gone to my grave without ever knowing what happened to Jeffrey.

Eleanor is the one person in the world who I believe loves Jeffrey as much as I do. During his infancy, when I was in greatest need, she was a thousand times more helpful and generous than Charlie or Mother or Father.

We all lived together, Eleanor and Charlie and Cha Cha, their adopted daughter, and Jeffrey and me, in their big, rambling old house. It was a full house—guppies and budgies and plants as big as trees and the iguana roaming underfoot, and the whole lot of us mostly ignored by old Ginger the cat, who spent his indolent days lying in the sun in the bay window or in front of the fireplace.

Eleanor was superwoman. She was raised to be that way. In the upstairs hall was a large hanging of a medieval knight elaborately embroidered by Eleanor's grandmother with the words "Stand therefore, having your loins girt about with truth" in a black arc above the knight's head. Eleanor's grandparents had been missionaries in Africa, and when her grandfather died Eleanor and other family members were at his bedside. In his last few moments, he clutched his Bible high over his head and said, "Victory, victory," then, smiling peacefully, he died.

"He was an honest and decent man," Eleanor said. Where other people praised their children for neatness and obedience, Eleanor's parents applauded the courage to be honest. "It's not just that honesty is the best policy," Eleanor would say. "It's a way of life. It's what my grandparents stood for. It set them apart."

The day I learned I was pregnant, Eleanor said we had to tell Mother and Father. I couldn't do it, so she did. She drove down to Juniper in the morning and was back the next day.

"What did they say, Eleanor? Were they terribly shocked? What did Father say?"

"Nothing much. He just kept shaking his head and saying, 'Oh dear dear dear. Oh dear.' I told him we'd take care of things."

I was clearly a disappointment to him. No first-class honours on my report card, no trophy for outstanding student of the year. "And what about Mother?"

"She made a pot of tea and she said, 'Huldah had such high hopes for Millicent.'"

"That was all? She was worried about what Granny Shelby would think?"

It was all too much for my parents—first Father's scandal, then mine. Several months later, they went to England to visit Granny Shelby. I knew they would not tell her about me. They were with Granny when Jeffrey was born.

Eleanor mothered me and the baby. She watched over him while I worked at The Piano House, giving lessons. Dinner was in the oven for me when I came home. She rocked Jeffrey to sleep in the cradle that used to belong to her father. She rubbed the cold teething ring on Jeffrey's gums. She held his hands when he took his first steps. She and Charlie wanted to adopt him. I said, "No."

Eventually I grew tired of having to be grateful. Charlie and I fought. He said I was like Father, inconsiderate and wilful. And then we moved out, Jeffrey and I, and lived in a rented room with a shared bathroom, and he cried for Eleanor.

"Whey Addie, Mama? Whey Addie go?"

"Auntie is at Auntie's house, Jeffy."

"Addie. Addie. Deffy go Addie."

And so I relented. Eleanor had said I could give piano lessons at the house and stay home with Jeffrey. We brought his boxes of toys into the living room. The more Cha Cha carried him away from the piano, the more he wanted to be there. He played "Twinkle Twinkle Little Star" with one finger. He could sing before he could talk. And he recognized music before he recognized words.

He was two and a half before Mother and Father finally saw him. They missed the most exciting days of his life, the time of transition from the universe to earth.

"Oh Millicent," Mother whispered when we all tiptoed upstairs and saw him asleep. "He's like you, isn't he, Father? There's that Shelby forehead." I could see, as she gazed at him, that she was genuinely thrilled. She put her finger to her lips and ever so lightly touched his cheeks.

Father said, "He should be baptized to make him really legitimate."

I looked at Father and said nothing.

"He's perfect the way he is," Eleanor said sharply. "What God has made perfect, let no man find wanting."

I tweaked Eleanor's arm gratefully but Mother glanced at her with displeasure. There were never any scenes or impertinences in our household.

When Mother and Father left, Eleanor turned to me and asked, "What has your father ever done for you, Millicent? Tell me that."

I frowned, trying to think of some instance of kindness directed solely towards me.

"You see?" she said. "Nothing. Zero."

"I've been fed and clothed," I said somewhat lamely. "What should one expect? We had tons of stuff. Good stuff. Books. Music. And fun. Isn't that what good parents give? Fun? He was never unkind."

"Are you blind, Millicent? That was a terribly unkind thing he said this afternoon. It was cruel."

"He didn't mean to hurt. I'm sure. He loves us. Don't you think he does, Charlie?"

Charlie groaned. "Wake up, Mills."

"You're pouring your love into a sieve," Eleanor added. "Just because he didn't beat you up—that's not love. Hitler couldn't stand the sight of blood either."

"Oh, what an awful thing to say. I know he loves us. I know you can't stand him but I really do love him."

"That is so sick, Millicent," Eleanor said. "It's so pathetic."

When I moved out for the second time, I did not return.

It wasn't easy being a single mother.

"Where's your dad?" one of Jeffrey's little friends asked him suddenly one day when he was in grade one.

"England," Jeffrey said.

"How come he's not here?"

"Because he has another family there."

"Are you going to see him?"

"When I grow up maybe." And Jeffrey ran around the room with his model airplane and crash-landed it on his teddy bear.

CHAPTER SEVENTEEN

When Jeffrey was twelve years old, I left him with Charlie and Eleanor for three insane and searing months. Dr. Jonathan Steele's divorce was pending. We had been corresponding for about six months. He told me he thought of me all the time. He wanted to see Jeffrey. I wrote that I would prefer to see him first, alone. I flew to Toronto, where he was working for six months, and took a taxi straight to his hotel room.

He wasn't expecting me. The room was littered with clothes, towels, newspapers, books and boxes of crackers. He had a paunch. His hair was thinner. He had a wad of cotton wool in his ear which he pulled out the moment he saw me.

"Camper Songbird! What a surprise! Oh, what a mess you've caught me in."

I should have trusted that first moment of mutual dismay. But before the evening was up, full-blown blindness had set in once more. I stayed with him the following night and the next and the next. I picked up his clothes. I nursed his infected ear.

We sang old songs. We made love in the shower and all day long.

The sweet and sticky madness lasted for three weeks. Then motherhood returned to me. This was not just my lover, this was the father of my son. I knew what I wanted. A complete family. And I wanted to be the wife my mother was not, a sexual partner who would satisfy every craving. The word "marriage" was first used by me.

"Of course. Yes, of course. But not immediately. It wouldn't look altogether right, Millicent. I presume you wouldn't want your good name dragged through the courts."

"It doesn't matter, Jonathan. Jeffrey is your real child, after all. So if I was named—"

"No. No, I couldn't let you."

The hesitation was the first sign that the waves were going to get choppy. That evening at dinner he said, "Your hair. . . ." He fluttered his hand dismissively. "Those braids make you look like a child. What is the image you are trying to present?"

And then, as my agitation increased, so did the more serious and threatening remarks.

"I find your mood swings difficult. There's no need to be depressed."

"But I am depressed."

"You sometimes strike me as rather unstable."

"You don't love me. You—"

"Nonsense. But if you think that's true, we shouldn't rush into things. Perhaps you should think about. . . ." He paused, searching for the right words.

"You're asking me to leave."

"Not at all. I'm suggesting it might be better if we took time to think. That we give serious thought to—to whether we are actually right for each other."

The boat was rocking wildly and it was time to jump. We'd had four intense weeks. There would be no moving to England. And in the meantime, thank God, Jeffrey was being spared the stormy weather. I congratulated myself that I had elected to chart the course before involving him. It was clear that Jonathan was not the sort of man who was interested in children. He hardly asked about Jeffrey.

From the time I knew it was ending, I discovered that I had little strength for the departure. In my mind I was back with Jeffrey in Edmonton, but my body was lingering on in Toronto. As I prepared to leave, he asked me to stay. So, like many a cling-on, I clung on. And on and on. We were on a roller-coaster ride. I did not raise the question of marriage again. He relaxed and was happier. I knew it was going nowhere, but the unhappier I became, the less able I felt to leave. And then with every passing day I began to feel a familiar dread.

On a Thursday afternoon, the doctor phoned to confirm the results. I had already called CARAL, the Canadian Abortion Rights Action League. They were on standby with all the arrangements. Dear Goddess, as I think back on it now, you must have been there with those efficient, understanding, anonymous women.

The one thought that brought me forcefully back to sanity was the realization that if I did not act at once I would soon be carrying a sentient being within me. Twelve years earlier, I had not known that I had a choice. That afternoon I wrenched myself forever out of the uncommitted arms of Dr. Jonathan "Skipper" Steele.

I didn't imagine, when I left without a word of explanation, that I would never see him again. I heard later that he called Eleanor and Charlie and that they were all frantic. They could not know that I was on an airplane headed for New York, or in a taxi on my way to the East Side Clinic, or in a waiting room with a half-dozen younger and older women whose eyes, like mine, were staring off elsewhere. I was on a table saying to the doctor that perhaps the test results had been mistaken, perhaps I wasn't really pregnant, perhaps an abortion wasn't really necessary.

"Oh you're pregnant all right," the doctor said. He was not unkind.

It didn't last long. Except for that one short, sharp moment when the cervix was dilated and the suction tube inserted, it wasn't unduly painful. I could not recognize the blood-red flurries travelling through the clear tube as anything other than bloody red flurries.

They did not let me rest long enough. I was nauseous and weak and faint when I was shovelled off the bed and made to sit in a chair. I was wearing the thickest sanitary pad I'd ever seen, and as soon as I could stand up, I took a taxi to the YWCA.

I phoned Eleanor, who said, "Good Lord, Millicent, we were so worried. Shall I come?"

"I'll be okay," I said, although I was anything but. I summoned whatever powers there are in the air for uprooted clinging vines and said, "Don't tell Jonathan where I am."

New York in July was unspeakable. I did not venture out into the muggy weather except for food and more pads. I lay in a pool of perspiration and loneliness, vowing that I would never, ever again pass judgement on anyone for anything.

CHAPTER EIGHTEEN

One gets used to things. In time the bizarre becomes familiar, the familiar assumes normalcy. In time one's jagged memories become rounded by the weather.

But certain mountain-peak moments remain. I've never forgotten the vow I made that stifling hot day in New York. "Judge not, that ye be not judged." Nor have I forgotten that earlier vow made in the depths of my adolescent soul. "I will never turn away from Father," I wrote in my diary, that earlier day. "The whole world can reject him, but I will not. Whatever has happened or whatever may happen, I will always love him. Never will I betray him. Never. This, I, Millicent Shelby, swear by all that is holy, until my beating heart stops and until forever after."

What endures is what endures. Some call it love. Some call it idolatry. Some call it denial. Some might say that I put myself under my father's spell. In the first instance, when I was fifteen, my need for love exceeded the need for truth. Charlie chose freedom. I chose the familiar. I chose to enter the dark mists of lies and pretence to stay with Father. With the promise I made to myself in New York, I aligned myself even more solidly with the condemned.

"You're so much like your father, Millicent," my mother had always said. It was true. Once I asked Father to hold out the palm of his hand and I compared our lines. They were alike. We were altogether alike. He had dark eyes. I had dark eyes. He was impetuous. I was impetuous. Father was weak, morally weak. So was I. I was my father's daughter through and through.

Charlie, who had never walked in the shoes of the accused, walked in the shoes of the accuser. In his eyes, I was a wilful and wanton woman. We slung mud at one another with mutual abandon.

"You're such a self-righteous pompous prig, Charlie. You have no idea what hurt you cause."

"And I suppose you do know the hurt you cause? You and Father? If you would stop to think for a change." Charlie, the perfect one who could do no wrong, looked down on me disdainfully.

"You think I got pregnant deliberately?"

"You're not a rag doll. There is such a thing as human volition."

I was so glad I no longer lived with Charlie. If it wasn't that Jeffrey needed Eleanor so much, I would have cut my ties and moved to the moon. The more Charlie was his mother's son, the more I defended Father.

Eleanor's phone call last autumn changed everything. When her long-distance fingers pried open my eyes, I was able to see at last that I could not see. If I was my father's daughter, who was the mother of my son?

That day she called, I was measuring the window for new blinds for this house—this big old inappropriate house Father bought when they decided to move to Ragland. Father had said he needed the space, but I saw it as a big box of trouble. The roof needed repair. The garden was a small jungle. I had made the decision to live with Father and Mother because they clearly needed the extra help, and because my apartment with its temperamental hot water system was inadequate. I had been used to bringing my laundry over here because it was handy and because, with Mother's incontinence, her sheets needed to be done almost every day.

I had finished the measuring and was upstairs in the shower washing my hair that afternoon when Father knocked on the door saying Eleanor was on the line. She and Martin had been visiting the day before. I took the call in my bedroom. "You've made it home all right, then?" Father hung up on the hall extension. I stood on the rug wet and cold, the shampoo stinging my eyes as Eleanor, her voice strained and tight, asked me how Jeffrey was.

"He's fine, I think. Why?"

Jeffrey was living with his partner, Lisa, in a flat in Battersea in England. I hadn't seen him in two years. We spoke every once in a while. Lisa was expecting their first baby, a boy according to the ultrasound. I was excitedly on my way to grandmotherhood.

"He's—he's all right, Millicent?"

"Of course he's all right." I couldn't imagine what she was worried about. She was going on and on about truth, her favourite topic. "What is it, Eleanor? What are you trying to say?"

"Millie. Oh Millicent. . . ." I could hear her breathing catch. She blurted it out in a gush of sobs. "I can't bear it. I can't. Our Jeffrey, Millicent. Our baby. His grandchild. It's monstrous!"

I couldn't know what I was hearing. I couldn't speak.

"Are you there, Millicent? Millicent, we have to call Jeffrey."

I took the big bath towel from around my body and, cradling the phone against my shoulder, I wrapped myself tightly, tucking the corner of the towel neatly under my arm. Then I crumpled to the floor. A voice outside me was whispering, "No," as I placed the receiver gently beside me and pushed it away. I listened to the loud beep beep beep and the mechanical voice telling me to "please hang up and try your call again."

I did try, again and again. I had to know. Jeffrey was never in. When I finally did reach him, I had control of myself. I sent a thousand prayers along the impossible long-distance line towards him. I summoned calmness and normalcy as I said, "I had a call from Auntie Eleanor, Jeff. She told me. . . ." He listened to me saying the unspeakable words. "Is it true, Jeff? Did he molest you?" And I heard him say, "I thought you knew, Mom. . . . It was nothing. . . ."

I got dressed and went downstairs. I could not look at Father. I could not stay in the house another moment. I left him standing bewildered at the window as I drove off without a word. I had no idea what to do except that I had to be somewhere else. I drove out of Ragland and onto the highway and kept going through the mountains and foothills and into the prairies, straight down the asphalt guillotine from small animal to small animal dead on the side of the road, one or two so small and crumpled I could not tell what they might have been—rabbit or cat or gopher.

What Father thought that day, I do not know. I drove till I came to the outskirts of a city. I walked among the unknown and unknowing people, facing neither praise nor judgement nor curiosity. Sweet anonymity. City of refuge with its department stores, clothes, candies, perfumes. I went to a faceless motel and paced and read the Gideon Bible. Deuteronomy 19. I lay on the stiff quilt on the bed and stared at the ceiling, watching the undulating dance of a cobweb's anchored shadow in the corner.

The power of denial I now know to be a wondrous defensive force against the massive assault of truth. Eleanor's call had ripped through my armour, but the reality of my father's betrayal could not completely kill some tiny persistent hope or need, I hardly know what to call it, some quietly desperate militant form of life that warred within me.

My journey towards more awareness has been through blindness, bondage, delusion, loathing, perhaps even love. The signposts in my heart have not always named the places where I have sat to rest. I still do not know what to call the tenderness that sometimes wells forth in me towards Father, even in the most soul-destroying moments. It may be a continuing form of denial. It may be love. I am to slay my fictions, I know, but I often do not know what my fictions are.

I stayed in the motel beyond the limit of my credit card. I can't remember when my skin-crawling revulsion began to subside. It was like a soundless curtain of mist rolling back onto the stage of my mind, a familiar mist obliterating distance and perspective. Ah, the comfortable blessed confusion in which there had been no requirement to judge. I summoned the gnat from its mouldy comforter to whisper its mouldy and comforting thoughts: perhaps it wasn't such a terrible thing. Jeffrey did say it was nothing. It was all a long time ago and my son was fine, he was more than fine. I did not need a gnat to remind me that the child who once was and the man he had become was a healthy, normal, sensitive person. Anyone could see that. He could not have been hurt. Martin was sure it had not hurt him either—people made too much of this sort of thing these days.

From within the churning cloud came the high bleating mewl of gulls, the white swoosh of traffic and the steady in and out of my breath as the greyness swirled its everyday past and I could see and not hear, I could hear and not see how my father busied himself as he had done all his life, connecting people to one another, connecting himself to them like laundry on the line, flap flap, windy words, connecting by hook and by crook, by pen and by phone and by tea party and every kind of event that his mind and convention allowed and did not allow. Father the networker, the social fabric maker, the fabricator.

Such is the need to be normal, the need to carry on in the day-by-day ordinary day, such is the desire to be like others, that I returned to the house in Ragland and concentrated on Mother's care. I said nothing to Father. I acted as if nothing were wrong.

CHAPTER NINETEEN

One wintry Sunday after my return, Father was a guest preacher at St. John's. He did not speak in abstractions. For him, God was indeed the Father, the One who loves unfathomably, the One who meets us where we are.

With his bright radio announcer's voice, he captivated the congregation. "Let me share with you one of the most significant moments of my long life," he began, and described a spring sunrise when he'd been in India, praying, gazing up at the mountaintops, at the deep purple glow on the white snow. "While I knelt there, marvelling at the grandeur, God shone across eternity and collided—God collided—with my soul." Father's fist smashed into the palm of his hand. "Just as surely as the sun's rays swept over the mountaintop that morning, God shone upon this tarnished vessel and God said to me, 'Barnabas, Barnabas, sinful and corrupt though you are, I claim you as my dwelling place.'"

Father paused and closed his eyes. "This is a mystery. How

can it be that the Lord of hosts would dwell in this most wretched of men?" His face shone with joy and assurance and grace. "And this—is this not good news? That Christ Jesus came into the world to save sinners? Dear friends, we all know the promise and the hope of God's presence. We have faith that He whom we do not see is with us. But in that moment, I did not have faith. I knew. I knew. God was fused in my soul. I knew in a way that I had never known before that our God of love and forgiveness was living in me and that I live because He lives. All my life, up to that moment, I had been a play actor saying the words.

"And so you see before you an old man who is retired, but a man who has hardly begun his spiritual climb. God is within us, my friends—each one of us, now and forever, no matter how lost we may think we are. 'For I am persuaded,' with St. Paul in Romans chapter eight, 'that neither death, nor life, nor angels, nor principalities, nor powers, nor things present, nor things to come, nor height, nor depth, nor any other creature shall be able to separate us from the love of God which is in Christ Jesus our Lord.'"

"I know he believes what he says," I told Charlie and Eleanor. "He really trusts that nothing we do can separate us from God. His soul is safe."

"Every wonderful sermon he gives is giftwrapped in a lie," Eleanor said. Charlie added that St. Paul had also said that to be carnally minded was death. Father would say anything for his own glory. Not true, I said. Not true. I put my faith in God's great power to redeem.

After Mother died, I gradually settled back into a slightly more active social life in Ragland, singing in the choir at St. John's, giving piano lessons, going to movies. Some days I would hear Father listening to old tapes of "Shelby Selects," his own rich voice singing the hymns of his Salvation Army youth. How many assassins, I wondered, would have had their hands stayed if they'd heard their victims singing familiar old songs?

When the old documentary about the first Juniper Centre was shown, I called up some friends and we watched it together.

"Your mother was so young! I love that hat. And your cute brother! What a picture-perfect family."

"What was it like, growing up with that much idealism?"

"Oh, isn't he vital! And so charismatic!"

The part of me that was discomfited fell into step with the old guard that marched proudly in the glow of the Shelby family parade. "Father is phenomenal. It's true. He really is."

But the next morning, as on many mornings, I wakened into the dullness and humidity of depression. I could not shake free of the wretched skeleton that had me by the throat, its bones clanking as it followed me about. The whole sordid past must never be made public. The night would consume us all if the vile deeds were known.

I did try, from time to time, to speak to Father. But I couldn't. Nor would the need to speak go away. Other worries rolled in and out of the mist—seabirds covered in thick oil spills, babies starving, the flies crawling along the lids of their eyes—the world was an unspeakable place. "I know it is," Eleanor said, "but we have to grow where we're planted. Our battle is right here in the family. The forces of deception are right here." Eleanor, with her phone calls, made the skeleton visible. She showed me that it was in command and that I was languishing in a dungeon of lies. Father too was there, locked up in his isolation cell.

Eleanor wanted to speak to Jeffrey and find out exactly where and when Father molested him, but I had told her firmly that she must not call. We had to wait for Jeffrey to bring it up himself, if he should ever want to. We wondered if it might have happened at some time during the months that I was away in Toronto, when Father, I understand, was up for a visit. Or it might have been that Christmas when Jeffrey and I went to Juniper. Jeffrey slept on the couch in Father's study. The possibility had not once, had not ever, entered my mind.

❖ ❖ ❖

The March sky was cloudless, the air unusually balmy, the morning Father called upstairs to ask if I'd accompany him on a trip to Ontario. He was to be guest of honour at the dedication ceremony of a new residential wing at the Juniper Centre in Chester Park. Wouldn't I like to see how the place had changed?

My friends were confounded. "What a great old guy your dad is," they said. "I hope I have half his energy when I'm his age."

"He's always had too much energy."

When the time came, dutiful daughter that I was, I parked my little life, packed my bags, set the answering machine and drove us to the airport. I held out my arm to support him as he got in and out of the car. I brushed the crumbs off his jacket.

The first night in Chester Park, we had dinner with other guests at the home of the new director and his family.

"Father Shelby. Wonderful to meet you, sir."

"Ah. The founder of the Juniper Centres. What a pleasure!"

Father loved it all. He ate like a hungry young man. He joked with the director's eleven-year-old son. Like many old people, he had become a talking machine. Throughout the evening, he preached, he bragged. He was the only one on stage, the only one in the universe. On and on he went, a *bon vivant* glorying in his many accomplishments, congratulating himself shamelessly, chuckling about the making of the documentary, about the way the money had rolled in.

It was years since Father had been in a situation like this. I couldn't think of how to stop him. I almost wished Charlie were there. He'd know how to handle it.

The eyes of the other guests around the table exchanged glances and glazed over. The hostess raised her eyebrows at her husband. One woman smiled indulgently throughout.

He's old, I told myself. It's forgiveable.

The company left early. Our host drove his mother-in-law home. I offered to help in clearing up the dishes.

Father turned to the child. Father's face was eager. As I stood up, his right hand reached over and tapped the boy's shoulder.

"Well, Jimmy," he said.

I watched, suddenly wary, as Father shifted his chair and leaned hungrily towards him. His left hand touched Jimmy's knee. Something inside me recoiled violently. Jimmy was wearing a short-sleeved shirt. "And what's this?" Father asked. "An airplane tattoo?" The boy squirmed as Father's palsied hand lifted his small arm to examine a picture of a little purple airplane on the inside of his forearm.

Then Father said, "Why don't you show me your room, Jimmy?"

I blanched. I could hardly breathe. It was all so clear. This was exactly the way it had happened before. Years earlier, I'd seen this exact same scene with other boys.

Then as now, I was like a bird mesmerized by a snake. I couldn't move. Father would take the boys to his study after dinner and close the door while the women washed up in the kitchen. How many times did this happen? Even after Father came back from his retreat in the mountains. I remembered the child in short pants who kept running in and out of the room, climbing on and off Father's lap. Then Father took the child's hand and led him away. One time I went to the study door. I turned the handle, but the door was locked.

How much evidence did I want? The genitals exposed? The eyes wide with shock? I had so much evidence that it was spilling out of the vault where it had been locked away for decades.

"Come," Father said, "let's go to your room."

They left the table hand in hand. They began climbing the stairs. With one hand tight against my pounding chest, the other on the table, I steadied myself.

"Is—is your washroom upstairs?"

"Yes, first door on the right."

I followed them, holding the railing for support, up the stairs, past the bathroom, leaning against the wall, past photographs of the family. Jimmy as a baby with soft rose-petal lips. Jimmy as a toddler.

So many photographs. The walls and shelves in Father's study were also covered with photographs. The Juniper Centres. Family pictures. Father with his arms around the shoulders of youths. And then there was the time I knocked over the lamp on his bedside table and found the clutch of snapshots of the special boys, the ones who, like himself, had dark hair, high foreheads, big round eyes and slightly hollow cheeks. His ideal child was himself, his own robbed innocence.

Father turned to close the door of Jimmy's room. I stood in the doorway.

"You can leave us, Millicent. Go and help in the kitchen." It was a direct order and it was forceful. Father, the honoured guest, was in command again. His springtime was upon him. His hand still rested on the child's small shoulder and Jimmy was looking down uncomfortably.

This child was almost twelve. Jeffrey had been twelve.

Jeffrey. Jeffrey.

"Jimmy, I—I need you to show me something," I stammered. I held out my hand. "Come with me."

The resolve in Father's eyes flashed briefly, then was replaced by what looked like sadness and a kind of pain, a kind of loneliness and need. He relinquished his hold.

I had no idea what I needed Jimmy to show me. We walked back downstairs together. He waited politely in the kitchen as I explained to our hostess that Father needed to rest. I called a cab to take us to the hotel.

I didn't sleep that night. Could I have been mistaken? Perhaps nothing would have happened. But the child could have been in danger. I had acted correctly. What was it that had happened to Jeffrey and Martin? I had to talk to Father. Eleanor was right. I had to. Father's hands had not willingly let go of the child.

I could imagine him defending himself. "They like what I do. It doesn't hurt them at all. I don't cause harm. It's pleasurable. It's good."

The following evening was the banquet. About two hundred people were present. Father, clean-shaven and presentable, basked in the warmth of the attention. The director rose from his seat beside him on the platform and went to the microphone. "Ladies and gentlemen, it is our great privilege to have with us, as our honoured guest tonight, the founder of the Juniper Centres. Please give our warmest welcome to the Reverend Dr. Charles Barnabas Shelby."

Father stood up, beaming and waving. The old magic was back. The audience were entranced, their eyes wide with delight.

I endured the evening. It was not an unfamiliar sensation— the pride and the shame, the truth and the lies. I was used to it all. But that evening, I could not shake off the chill of the night before. It was not Father but a corpse on stage, its putrid flesh dressed in fine robes and silks, parading about. I could not stop the stench.

"Wonderful, wasn't it, Millicent! They loved me." He babbled happily all the way back to the hotel. He had enchanted the guests with his charm. He had entertained them with a joke and a song. He, the living nightmare in my life, his jaw unhinged, had lapped up the applause. And now that we were alone together, he was expecting me to continue the charade.

I could not do it. I could not look at him. I had needed a different kind of evening. The truth, for once. I needed a repentant man. I needed him to cover himself in sackcloth and ashes and to beat his breast and wail, "Lord, I have sinned against heaven and against Thee and I am not worthy to be called Thy child. I have abused and molested your children. I have betrayed a holy trust."

But Father had never made such lamentations. Never.

The following week, we were guests at a retreat centre. He was to give the homily that Sunday. On Saturday I could no longer contain the turmoil.

CHAPTER TWENTY

On Saturday afternoon, Father was resting on the couch in the retreat centre's large common room. We had been driven seventy-five miles over rocky country roads, over hills and streams, to the rough log structures in the woods. A portly, smiling man greeted us and showed us to our rooms. The toilets were outside. The water was cold.

I spent the morning walking among the trees. In that place of peace, I was not at peace. I thought about Jimmy and Jeffrey. And I thought about Father. My hypocritical, repulsive, gentle Father.

He was lying on his back on the couch opposite a huge fireplace, tapping the tips of his fingers together and staring at the dark, beamed ceiling.

"People are so wonderful," he said to me quietly as I came in. "They are so good to me, so good to me."

I sat in an armchair opposite him.

"What do you think Jesus meant," I began, "when he said,

'Things that were hidden will be shouted from the rooftops'?"

He stopped tapping his fingers and turned his head slightly in my direction.

"'The truth, the way, the life,'" I said. "The truth, Father."

He looked at me enquiringly.

It may have been five more minutes and I didn't speak. My mind was a cauldron of the unsaid. All my life I had dreaded the explosive power of anger. Like my mother before me, I had learned to fear it.

There had been so much destruction in the world in the name of truth. The Inquisition. The Crusades. Over the years, I had told myself that I would not speak until I knew that Love was speaking. Ours was a gentle house. I would wait for gentleness. But that afternoon, I did not stop for that consideration. I said the words.

"I know about Jeffrey, Father. I know the truth. I know what you did."

Father looked straight at me and there was not a flicker of recognition in his eyes.

"That you—that you—touched him."

There was no change of expression as he turned his face away. His voice was quiet, almost timid. "How old was he?"

"Twelve."

The words were said. I had picked up the knife. I had plunged it straight down. What was I expecting? The sky to fall? The earth to open up and swallow us?

It appears that the essence of who I am is someone who does not easily bear pain. Whether out of cowardice or misplaced kindness I do not know, but I leapt in at that juncture to rescue him from whatever redemptive work might have been accomplished from his facing the pain in me. I said, "Jeffrey said it didn't harm him."

He nodded. He looked relieved. Nothing more was said. The lid was firmly back on Pandora's box again. But an imp had been released and sat on his chest. He did not speak to me. He closed his eyes. He looked as if he was in prayer. And then he fell asleep. When he wakened, he was not his normal bubbly self.

The next day, he stood in the pulpit of the chapel and delivered a familiar, old-fashioned sermon—the story of his conversion—Jesus as alive, as present, as appearing to him when he was ill. Jesus the healer. Jesus the forgiver. Jesus the comforter, who, even at the moment of greatest extremity, as he hung dying on the Cross, turned to his beloved disciple, John, and asked him to care for Mary, his grieving mother.

"His mother. . . . Mother," Father repeated. "Mother . . . Mother." His two hands held the sides of the pulpit. He bowed his head. "In the name of the Father and of the Son and of the Holy Ghost. Amen." He turned and stepped down slowly. It was not the usual way he ended that sermon.

After the service, the small congregation went outside onto the lawn to have coffee. A chair was brought for Father. I watched him sitting there quietly, nodding, not speaking, not engaging in the easy banter. I asked if he wanted to go and rest and he nodded.

He slept all afternoon. When he got up I asked if he was all right. He smiled at me and blinked his eyes. "God is telling me I am talking too much," he said. That was the last thing he said that day.

By noon the next day I knew that something was wrong. The non-stop self-aggrandizing which had become irritating background noise had changed to one-syllable responses to questions. He was pale and weak. He ate his supper mechanically.

"What's wrong, Father?"

No answer. A smile. A wink.

"We should leave tomorrow. You should see your doctor."

Another smile.

We were expected to stay the week. I explained the situation to our hosts. I retired early that night to my simple room with its single bed, coat rack, desk and chair, a room with the window open to the moonlight and the pines and the occasional sound of wild animals.

CHAPTER TWENTY-ONE

It was while I slept in that austere room in the middle of the wilderness that I had the dream—a dream I do not now remember except for the statement that arose from it: the Goddess of Mercy is the Goddess of Abundance.

Thus, my Goddess, began the journey towards you—the search for the pathway to your throne, the watchfulness for signs of an abundant universe. I looked for you everywhere, in conversations, in connections between generosity and the capacity to forgive.

The doctor said Father had suffered a mild stroke. I asked if it could have been brought on by emotional trauma and he shrugged. "Maybe," he said. I blamed myself. I blamed the imp. I threw my arms around Father as he lay in his hospital bed and told him I loved him.

"I'm so sorry," I whispered as he lay suddenly mute, staring at his hands.

Did I need to be the agent of judgement? I asked myself. The

dream had directed me towards mercy, and here was mercy—
that I had acted to slay the dearest man in my life, but he was
still alive—enfeebled and diminished, but mercifully alive. And
I was being taught, through my remorse, that judgement was
not required of me. "Vengeance is mine. I will repay," saith the
Lord. The universe would unfold as it would.

I feared there might be another stroke. Flesh was weak. I
took Father home. He needed care. I cleaned and shopped and
cooked. I shaved him whenever he went out or when there was
company, otherwise he shaved himself and bits of stubble were
left on his chin and neck. I wiped the food off the floor around
his chair after every meal.

As the weeks passed, his speech gradually returned. In the
evenings, we watched the news together. Stories on child abuse
were erupting across the continent. We didn't discuss them.

And then, one night, there was a short item about Mother
Teresa. I sat and watched steadily as the champion of the
poorest of the poor assailed me. She had done so before. The
other time had been when Father and I were at the retreat
centre in Ontario. Mother Teresa had arrived on the cover of a
magazine, her stern unsmiling face sharp with judgement. It
was the night following Father's stroke and I was unable to
sleep. I was in the lounge, sitting in a big leather armchair by
the fireplace, looking through a pile of magazines. I carried a
few of them to my room and put them on the floor. As I turned
the pages, I was thinking of the words I'd spoken to Father, how
I'd tried so ineffectually to lance the festering wound in my
heart, and how, almost immediately, he had been stricken.

As I wandered down the labyrinthine ways of sleeplessness
and anxiety, there staring up at me from the floor in that bare

room was Mother Teresa. And for the first time in years, I thought about my abortion and the baby who had not been born.

Mother Teresa. Gatekeeper of the dying. Winner of the Nobel Peace Prize. Paragon of virtue.

I knew that I, Millicent Shelby, stood judged by her to be a greater criminal than my father. I was a destroyer of the most innocent holy charge entrusted to my flesh, a murderer of my own sacred child. The punishment for this most heinous crime was death. Had she not herself said as much on Parliament Hill in Ottawa? And was she not as potent an authority on good and evil as the world had to offer? She surely had access to verities hidden from moral degenerates like me. To be subject to her world view was to dwell in the most paralyzing judgement, was to be crushed alive under a mountain of guilt. All night long, her disembodied head pronounced the death penalty over me: I had desecrated the holiest of holies, the safest inner sanctum. I had uprooted the seed and the seedling, the growing shoot of a human soul. Small wonder that my dreaming mind fled from the banner of her Lord and King and sought instead the Goddess of Mercy, ancient assuager of suffering.

At the time of the abortion, I did not name the rapidly organizing cells within me. To my eyes they were human cells, akin to other living human cells, wondrously alive with genetic coding. But I did not weight their existence with consciousness. For me, human tissue was sacred only in the way that all life was sacred. I did not elevate the non-sentient above the sentient. Far greater, to my mind, was the suffering of a drowning mouse than the dissembling of an embryo that had no pathways of pain. Suffering was my starting point in questions of good and evil. In a universe beyond the reaches of the human imagination I could not guess what torments there might be beyond death, before birth, in other forms of consciousness. The charge that abortion was murder lay for me in a world of abstraction, and in theories of sacredness. On that Thursday afternoon in Toronto, after the call from the doctor, the dread of delay was so great that I did not even think.

If I had to, I would do it again. I would take the leap of faith out of the edifice of the patriarchs and into the blessed company of pro-choice.

We are a planet of mortals who stumble about with our murderous convictions. In the name of the weak, for the sake of the weak, we murder the weak. Look, Mother Teresa, upon this prison cell where I hide among pedophiles and other uncomprehending criminals. I am placing my case beside that of my father's, and wait for the judgement of mercy.

CHAPTER TWENTY-TWO

The days have been grey, neither dark nor bright. Grey, it seems to me, is the colour of mercy. A grey sky, grey trees, grey mountains, all bleeding into one another. A glimmer of filtered light at both midnight and noon. Blessed sufficiency.

Often, in the afternoons, we sit on the front porch in wicker chairs with our cups of tea, noting the new blooms in the garden and watching the passing parade—Boots, our black and white cat, and the neighbour's tabby cat chasing each other, chasing the squirrels and the birds. We love the birds, the robins, the jays, but most especially we love the barn swallows.

I didn't measure their days. I didn't note the first day we saw the first barn swallow bringing the twig to the porch, but we congratulated ourselves on our good luck.

"Look, they're building a nest right here on the porch!" I exclaimed to Father. "How wonderful."

He said he had noticed them already from the living-room window early one morning, as they flew swooping and diving back and forth across the front lawn.

"Let's not use the front door," I suggested, "until they're established. Let's not sit outside for a while."

And so every day—was it in late June or early July that they began, darting back and forth like the swallows they were, brown and black and small and sleekly beautiful with their pointed tails and their swift, silent flight day after day, swoosh up to their pinpoint landing on the corner at the top of the pillar beneath the porch roof.

At first we watched them through the peephole in the front door, and we could see them as if far away at the end of a long telescope, the two tiny dark shapes, one after the other, packing their grey nest into shape. Sometimes we'd see the two of them sitting together. Then bit by bit we got them used to us standing motionless in the doorway. We noted that there was one particular spot on a telephone wire where one swallow would sit keeping guard.

And then came the day when, the nest completed, we began using the front door again and the birds did not fly away. For how many days did they sit there? A week maybe. I didn't want to disturb them by climbing up on a chair to see if there were eggs inside. A bird was almost always in residence. The white sloping pillar began showing signs of their presence. Besides the twigs on the porch floor, there were now round and curled bird droppings on the bench and along the pillar, which, on the rare occasion when the birds were not there, I would sweep away.

One afternoon we saw them sitting by turn on the edge of the nest, peering in, fussing, their heads turning this way and that. And the next day, or the day after, there were whitish shells on the ground. And we knew the babies had been born, but so as not to frighten them we stood watch from our safe distance.

A short while later, we saw the most idiotic little grey tufts and furry little wobbly things moving. It was amazing how fast they grew. They looked so wonderfully ugly—tiny aliens, their funny yellow beaks big as all creation, yawning open soundlessly. That's all we could see at the top of the nest—beaks, beaks and no feathers. I wasn't sure how many there were.

All work stopped as we spent the days watching and admiring the tireless parents zooming in for the endless day-long feedings. I followed their outbound flight as they sped high and low along the treetops and lawns towards a soccer field two blocks away. There, with other swallows, they hunted for flying insects.

For a few days we thought there were four babies, but one day I counted five. It was all miraculous and joyful. I knew we'd get up one morning and we'd see them doing their practice flight. We saw the beaks starting to change, the tips getting darker. The grey tufts began to show some brown. And then the funny things began to preen themselves, lifting their stubby, featherless wings.

At first, when the babies were nothing but yellow beaks, they'd open them at any sound. A cough, a footstep, the door closing. Gradually they learned to discriminate. It was their parents' cheeps as they landed on the nest that made them respond with their own chirps. Every few seconds or minutes they were fed and the racket increased.

"What a wonder it all is," I said to Father. We were both enthralled. We kept Boots indoors.

Then one morning when we looked up, we saw that three of the babies were gone. Out in the garden we saw the evidence—two dead on the lawn, one in the jaws of the neighbour's tabby cat.

We were desperate. Two babies were still left. I thought of creating a chicken-wire structure around the base of the pillar so that the tabby would not be able to approach. I thought of hanging cloth and tacking it in an arc beneath the nest. Eventually I settled for an intricate series of booby traps for the cat, balancing concrete blocks delicately along the bench beneath the pillar so that, if the cat leapt up in an effort to launch itself up to the two remaining babies, it would find itself clawing air.

It worked. The first night I heard a block thud to the porch. I ran out and saw the wretched beast on the other side of the street, its tail twitching nervously. I improved the traps, the next day adding trays of water. The following night there was another thud. Out I rushed again in my nightie. No cat in sight.

Father sat guard over the front porch, his broom beside him, ready to shoo away the predator. I brought his lunch and tea out for him on a tray. The cat was lurking about, eyeing the nest, eyeing the broom and Father.

"A good thing you're standing guard," I said.

The following afternoon, when I got back from the drug-store, one bird was down on the porch floor. Father was standing with broom in hand, frightening both parent birds and cat.

I picked up the baby and lifted it back into the nest with the other survivor. That may have been a mistake. The birds and their nest were infested with hordes of tiny, tiny lice that moved faster than the fastest spiders I have ever seen. When I placed a stick near the nest, it was immediately swarmed. My hands and arms and neck and shoulders felt a maddening itch. I rushed upstairs and showered.

Both babies died, one after the other, that day. Their parent birds did not abandon them. It may have been the lice. The summer of the miracle had become the summer of sadness. Father sat quietly all afternoon.

"What a pity, what a pity," he repeated softly. He didn't want to invite anyone for tea and he didn't want to go out for his weekly visit with a couple who lived in a group home nearby.

"I'm a sentimental old man."

We ate supper in silence.

Late that night, Father called to waken me. "Come and see, Millicent. Come and see. Bring your camera."

I descended the stairs to a sweet, musky fragrance, a light perfume pervading the living room. The night-blooming cereus, that awkward plant with its tough cactus leaves and its long, ungainly stem touching the ceiling, was finally in flower.

"Isn't it astonishing, Millicent? Oh, if Mother could see this! What an uncommonly beautiful flower it is."

I placed the camera on a tripod and took several shots. Mother had been tending that plant for ten years. Now, for the first time, it was in flower. On the very day that the baby birds died, layers and layers of long, thin white petals were opening like frilly skirts and a cascade of jungle incense filled the room. It lasted for almost an hour. Then it was over.

CHAPTER TWENTY-THREE

Father does not talk about the baby birds. Father is habituated to positive thinking. He calls friends and talks about his flower. He framed the best photograph and tells guests over and over how he has been caring for the plant for so long.

"It's Meredith's gift, you see. I'm so blessed," he says. "God is so good to me—that He has allowed me to live to see His beautiful night-blossom."

Father's complete recovery from his stroke has been remarkable. He is a man who has recovered from every illness and accident in his life. Some call it a miracle. Others say it is faith at work. One parishioner at St. John's said, "Well, he's obviously living right."

The people from St. John's drop by frequently, and Father the raconteur charms his guests with tales of his daughter's devotion. As his self-congratulatory speeches again dominate the airwaves, my irritation sometimes surfaces. A kind of early-morning soul weariness assails me these days. I find myself turning into my mother with her fixed, long-suffering smile. Sometimes I can hardly hold back my disgust as he basks in his own praises.

On two occasions recently, I've tried to ask what he did to Jeffrey. Repelled though I am by it all, I tell myself that, however perverted he may be, he is not in any way a violent man—possibly Jeffrey was right and it was a brief moment's touching, and just one time. It's possible that he did not do lasting harm. But Jeffrey was a particularly sensitive, intelligent child. And he was so impressionable.

One early Saturday morning after a sleepless night, I phoned Jeffrey and broached the subject again, as delicately as I could. "I'm worried about what happened to you," I said, "that time when you were twelve."

"You worry too much, Mom."

"What do you feel about what Grandad did? What do you feel about him?"

"Oh, he's a great guy." The answer came back too quickly, straight out of his mouth, not from the heart, not from the body.

"Don't you think he's a hypocrite?"

A pause this time. "Well, we're all hypocrites, aren't we?"

"But you don't believe the things he stands for. The church. The Bible. Faith. Any of those sorts of things."

I could imagine the quizzical look on his face, half amused, half challenged. Jeffrey has a way of sidestepping heavy questions by making light of them. "Hmm. Well." A light chuckle. "I guess you're right about that. Maybe he did me a favour. We can get along pretty well without all that religious baggage, don't you think?"

A favour? I wanted to cry out. He did you a favour by betraying you? It's good that you've turned away from the rich world of stories that could guide you on a journey towards freedom? Jeffrey, no, it wasn't a favour, I wanted to shout. Instead, I said quietly, "I don't know what to think, Jeffy." My way was not Eleanor's way. I was not the sort of person who rocked boats. I let the conversation drift to other things.

◆   ◆   ◆

A few weeks ago, Father and I were watching the news together. Two Roman Catholic brothers were being charged with sexual abuse of boys.

"What do you think about that, Father?" I lowered the volume slightly with the remote control.

He nodded gravely. "Vengeance is not a good thing," he said quietly. "No. Not good at all." He was obviously concerned for the two brothers and had not a thought for the boys. No mention of trust or betrayal. After a moment, he added, "The problem is celibacy. It's a harsh measure. Much too harsh. It's not natural."

"But you were married," I blurted out.

His head dropped forward a little. "Yes." After a moment, he added, "Mother—certainly Mother was a wonderful woman. Certainly, she was. But"—he shifted in his armchair and looked obliquely in my direction—"can you understand? She was completely without those feelings."

I remembered Mother turning aside when I asked her about sex. With a look of distaste, she'd said, "Sex is an animal thing." Mother was decidedly prudish. For years I had believed that

Father's deviant behaviour was partly, if not altogether, Mother's fault. Poor Mother. There was no point in arguing the matter now. Wherever she was, she was beyond false accusations.

"Do you think you have been forgiven, Father?"

"God came into the world to save sinners, and I am a sinner."

"But don't sinners have to turn from their sins? The Bible says you have to repent and *turn*. Do you think it was God's fault? God just didn't help you? Why did He not give you the strength to resist the temptation?"

Father turned back to the TV. The news had changed to the story of a lost child. "Those are the sorts of questions humans ask," he said, "but God has all the answers. God knows everything."

He was dismissing me, I thought. At the same time, it was a kind of answer to say he did not have an answer. It seemed he was leaving the matter to God. He got up to go before the news was over. "God is love," he said as he shuffled away. "God is love."

A parrot could say as much, I thought.

I didn't raise the subject again for a few days, but questions continued to obsess me. What did he think love was? I worried about his state of mind. Had he ever repented? Did he know that what he had done was wrong? His complete lack of remorse was puzzling. And chilling. Could he, who seemed to have no conscience in that one area, have a healthy conscience otherwise? What monstrous mockery of faith was it that allowed him to experience forgiveness without turning from his sin? Or was forgiveness his word for licence?

Once more I approached the subject. It was Sunday morning and we were driving home from church.

"About the past, Father, and the boys. I don't know how many there were. I don't know what you did. I'm just wondering—do you think they were harmed?"

"Oh, I don't suppose so. No. They're all living quite happy lives, I believe."

"How do you know?"

No answer.

"You didn't think you were doing wrong?"

Again, no reply. When I parked the car, he fumbled his way out of the seatbelt by himself and made his way to the house. "Father, you didn't think you were doing wrong?"

His voice trembled as he said, "Why are you persecuting me, Millicent? It's all so long ago."

He struggled as quickly as he could to the front steps and climbed, holding the railing, one step at a time, like a toddler. Old age is a time of such vulnerability. It seemed to me, as I watched him making his way unsteadily, that accosting him with my wounding questions was in some ways like child abuse. I didn't want to be a bully. He was frail and in his dotage and it was all just too late.

After that Sunday's non-conversation, I didn't think I would question him again. It was so hopeless and pitiful. He was an old man now, I told myself, and the right and loving thing would be to let him spend his last days in his own way, with his own conscience or lack of conscience directing him. I had tried to speak to him. I had tried and tried. I had done enough. It was time to close the book. I would just have to make sure he was not left alone with boys.

And then Eleanor called. She had news about Martin from her sister, Stephannie. They were in San Francisco. Martin had been found unconscious on the floor.

"What? What happened?"

"It's not the first time, Millicent. He made one other suicide attempt in Sweden."

"No! I had no idea, Eleanor. Did you know that about him before? Why didn't you tell me? He seemed so strong, and so sure of himself. It couldn't have had anything to do with Father, could it? He said he didn't blame Father. His parents got divorced when he was quite young, didn't they?"

"Stephannie wants to bring charges."

"Against Father? My God, that would kill him."

"Kill Father! What about Martin? Think about Martin, Millicent! He has just tried to kill *himself!*"

Eleanor called again in the middle of the night. I was dreaming of a brown ball the size of a quail's egg lodged in my ear. I didn't believe what she was saying.

"The new rector at St. Chad's? Oh no. Father couldn't have done anything like that. He couldn't have."

"Ask him."

CHAPTER TWENTY-FOUR

I've set the small, round table in the sunroom for afternoon tea and scones. Mother's favourite Mozart is playing softly in the background. The room is full of flowering plants, hanging ferns, spider plants. The afternoon sun beams through the leaves.

"Father, how are you feeling?"

"I'm very well, thank you." He stirs the milk with his special teaspoon, once, twice, and places it shakily in the saucer.

"This strawberry jam is quite good, isn't it?"

"Lovely and thick. Yes."

"Not quite as good as Mother used to make."

Father is relaxed. I butter the scones for him. We sip our tea in silence. Finally, I sigh deeply and lean towards him. "There are some things I need to ask you, Father. Some serious things—because I need your help. I know how you have felt sometimes—that I was persecuting you. But Father, I never— never ever—wanted to hurt you. I know you never wanted to hurt anyone either. All my life, you must know this, I've loved you so much. And right now, because—because I'm in pain, I need to ask you some things. Is that all right?"

He looks blankly at me.

"Shall I pour you another cup of tea?"

He nods.

Once again, the milk, the stirring, once, twice, the shaking off of the drops, his hand unsteady with the palsy of old age.

"Have you ever talked to anyone about—about the boys—about the sex? Have you ever told anyone the whole story? Everything?"

He looks down at the table and shakes his head slightly.

"I need to ask you about yourself. My pain is because I don't understand."

He doesn't respond.

"That time you'd been away from home so long. You were at the Juniper Centre up north. That was the time you were caught and sent home. And you saw the bishop."

There is no expression on his face.

"Is it something that happened most when you were travelling?"

He nods.

"It started when you were quite young?"

"Yes."

"Did something happen to you? When you were a boy, I mean—what age?"

"Around eight, I think. An older boy."

"Were you frightened? Was it pleasurable?"

"Oh, I was very frightened. And yes—yes it was—pleasurable at the same time. Frightening but pleasurable."

"What did he do? Do you think that started the whole thing?

Changed your life? Or maybe—were you—do you think maybe you were born that way? Some people think people are born that way."

Is there the slightest brightening? His eyes lift upwards as he nods. "I have always thought I was different. Even as a small child, I didn't like all the fighting."

"That older boy. Did he—did he penetrate you?"

"No. Nothing like that."

"He just touched you?"

No response.

"And other experiences?"

"After that first time—yes, I started to do the same sorts of things—with other children. And, well, I had a friend—the son of a clergyman—he was my own age. He said he'd follow me to the ends of the earth."

"And then you went to India. And you came to Canada."

"Yes."

"It was mostly with young men? Is that right?"

"Yes."

"Things have changed so much since you were young. I mean, if we think about homosexuality. People say it's not such a terrible thing these days. Maybe—do you think maybe it'll be that way about children someday? Not such a terrible thing?" My question is a ruse. I need him to sense no judgement if I am to learn the truth.

"I don't know."

The whole truth, Eleanor said last night, may never come to light.

"Did you ever . . . Father, did you ever have anal sex with . . . with. . . ?" How can I be asking this? Please God, let him say no. Let it be that he only touched the boys for perhaps the briefest second, that maybe he patted their behinds and let them go, that he did not frighten or startle or hurt them. I cannot believe he would hurt anyone. Jeffrey said he didn't hurt him.

He looks away.

"Father, I don't mean to embarrass you. But I want to understand. Can you help me? Didn't St. Paul say we must bear one another's burdens? If you've never told anyone—it must be such a great burden for you."

He nods.

"More tea?"

His folded hands touch his forehead and his eyes are closed. Is he praying?

"Father, can you tell me—did you ever have anal sex? Eleanor went to talk with the new rector at St. Chad's yesterday, Peter Bowles. Do you remember Peter Bowles? He said you approached him when he was a young seminarian."

"Peter Bowles?"

"Is it true? Did you try to have anal sex with him? Did you, Father? Did you ever do that with other boys?"

His eyes still closed, he nods his head slowly. "Yes. There was that."

My hand shakes as I put the teapot down. Father has admitted to this. He has actually done this. What have I been thinking all these years? What on earth did I think those two words meant? *Sex. Boys.* The truth is, I did not think. I did not ever imagine what he might actually have done.

"And when you were up north. How many boys were you involved with?"

"About . . . thirty maybe."

Thirty! My God! Thirty! That means there were more. He admits to thirty!

I have to carry on with this. There may never be another opportunity. I am struggling for self-control and I register no change in my tone of voice. "And you—fondled them? Just once?"

Why am I saying this? I already know it was more than fondling.

"Mostly just one time."

"With some, it was more than one time?"

"Yes."

"And they were how old?"

"Around twelve perhaps. Twelve. Fourteen. Twenty. Mostly around twenty. I—I loved them."

"And you said there was anal penetration."

"There was that."

How can I be sitting here in this sunny room? How can my voice be functioning? How is it that I am not rising out of my seat in revulsion?

"And in the mouth?"

"No. Nothing like that."

"One time, Father—" I remember this suddenly. I remember that very small child. Both his parents were right there as well. "One time, after you came back from the North and the church fell apart, I saw you with a little boy. He was under five. Three maybe. Or four. He was on your lap. Even children that young?"

Just the slightest nod. One movement.

"And after you spoke with the bishop, it still continued."

Another slight nod.

"To this very day. You could still. . . ."

"I haven't done. . . ."

"But the urge. . . ."

"Yes."

"And Charlie, Father? Charlie too?"

"No. No."

"Not when he was little? Too little to remember?"

"No. Not Charlie."

"But Martin. Martin was up at Juniper North that summer, at the camp."

"I don't remember."

"He was one of them. Did you penetrate him?"

"No."

"But what did you do?"

"You'll have to ask him."

"He has been asked. He said you came to him at night and you put your hands under the blanket. . . ."

✧   ✧   ✧

Lord, this is an abandoned planet. No guardian angels have been here to stay the hands of those who harm. I shall never be able to doubt again that harm was done. Great and severe and lasting harm. I cannot ask any more questions. The torment of not knowing enough has been replaced by the torment of knowing too much. I have sunk my teeth into the fruit of the knowledge of evil. The small gnat lies dead in my hand—that whispering tiny hope that did once so temptingly flit through my mind. I have killed it with the stone that my heart now is.

I have tried to understand. I have failed to understand. I have come to the day when I doubt Love so thoroughly that I hardly know why I bother. I am praying because there is nothing else for me to do, like someone buried alive in the earth, waiting for death, and praying because there is nothing else to do.

In the crucible of this hour, ashes are blowing. Through the prism of prayer, the rain ascends.

CHAPTER TWENTY-FIVE

My father, we have lived for too long under the domination of the Father of Lies. In choosing to satisfy your lust you did not choose understanding. In choosing to be your defender, I chose not to see your villainy. You defiled the most fragile, most precious treasures entrusted to your care—the not-yet-formed minds of the young. You altered forever the rich and beautiful patterns of their thoughts. You took the pastel shadings of their dreams and splashed crimson and dung across the canvas of their innocent days. You swooped upon the sheltered nests of infant birds, their beaks open, their heads awkwardly angled upwards in a trust as large as the sky. With your unseeing hunger, you plucked the trust from their upturned faces and fed yourself till you could eat no more. Thirty children, Father? There must have been hundreds.

You were no ordinary wolf in sheep's clothing. You dressed yourself in the robes of the Good Shepherd and stole God's lambs. In the sacred soil of their young lives you planted moral confusion, the world as not safe, symbols as untrustworthy, God as betrayer. You made them to lie down in green pastures, you led them by still waters and devoured their souls.

It's the mothers that I hear, scratching at the soil, screaming to know where their little boys lie. It's their broken hearts and their self-recrimination that they trusted blindly and did not protect their sons. And here Father lies in his old age, in his rocking bed, as the wind blows, as the bough bends, and down comes the house at last, Father, with Charlie and Mother and me and cradle and all.

Spirit of holiness, ". . . we have erred and strayed from Thy ways like lost sheep, we have followed too much the devices and desires of our own hearts, we have offended against Thy holy laws, we have left undone those things which we ought to have done and we have done those things which we ought not to have done"—perpetrators and bystanders that we are— "and there is no health in us."

I fed the monster on the flesh of my child. I turned aside as he engorged himself on other children. Deliver me from the nightmare of my life.

There are so many stories of betrayal in the world. This is one. There are so many hells. This is one. I have been brought down to this particular hell, into the liquid fire, into judgement and despair.

To whom and to what did those children turn after my father tossed their small bodies aside? To castles like mine, made of wind and dust, to bottles, to needles, to many forms of speechlessness, to the quick thrust of their loins into the unloved bodies of other children without history.

All my life I have been asleep, rocking among stones full of groans too deep for uttering. I am heaving myself awake, filled now with the drumbeat of murderous thoughts. I wish him to be dead. Release me, oh, from this cauldron of his crimes.

It is your feet, dear Father, that have danced on the grave of God the Father. You trampled the faith of the faithful. You silenced the children. But Father, truth, like the water level, rises and floods the basement while you sleep. You say you did not think you were doing harm. Indeed, you did not think at all of the boys, of their parents. You did not think of the community of the faithful or of the ability to trust, which is the foundation of health. You did not think of Mother or Charlie or me, Father Judas, as you betrayed the innocent with your unholy kisses.

You have made the white dog-collar uniform a sign of the abhorred. You belong to the army of child molesters, of pederasts and pedophiles, of the perverted and the deceitful. We see a priest rounding the corner of the street and we shudder. We see him at an airport or in a taxi or entering a building and a cloud of suspicion and disgust descends over us. We are made ill by your presence.

As I stone you, dear Father, I am stoning your Father, and I am stoning my love, and here lies an unholy trinity, dead and dead and dead.

Until you acknowledge the depths of your depravity, you will not waken to the cleansing flames. Until you walk into the field of fire, you will find no angel of mercy.

Not in the love of his daughter is mercy to be found for my father. I will not be applying to join the company of angels, mere mortal that I am. Nor will I any longer this day mewl for the defence. I am flung weeping from that once-upon-a-time when I loved the idea of my father, when I tried to create the idol I adored, when I worshipped a lie. That is finished. It is finished. I am leaving the courtroom now. But as I rush headlong out the door, stumbling in my haste to get away, I am followed by the long shadow of his life.

Who is to pay the impossible debt my parent has incurred? Unto the third and fourth generation, I am told, the children's children are in chains. Behold your legacy, Father. You have sold us into bondage.

Have mercy, oh Goddess, on the innocents.

On the innocents, oh Goddess, have mercy.

The way of truth is the way of the light. I am seeking the light after my lifelong night. I am telling the untellable to myself, to others, in whispers, in intimate conversation. And with every breath in my body I am striving to be free, that the child of my child may be strong and truthful and unashamed.

CHAPTER TWENTY-SIX

And so, Eleanor, I have come stumbling and exhausted to the altar of telling. The long silence has seeped out of my finger-nails, out of my dried tear ducts. I am wrung dry.

Morning after morning, I have been waking to a spiralling journey, down into the whirlpool of revulsion and out and around and down again. I have sought the Goddess the way a starving beast seeks food. Madly. Faster than the speed of light, she has been hastening my way, catching me even as I tumble and fall. She has required of me only this: to seek her face.

After Father's disclosure I went to see Charlie and Eleanor. "Put him in a seniors' home," Eleanor said, "and move back here. If you don't want to live with us I'll help you find an apartment. You've got more friends here than in Ragland."

"I'd like to—but—but—I can't just throw him to the dogs. Can you imagine if people found out?" I asked.

I was back within a week. The dishes were unwashed and the kitchen floor was sticky with spilled milk around the cat's bowl. The house smelled foul. Father didn't say a word to me about having gone. I followed him out to the garden in the afternoon and waited for him to be finished watering. My need to know more was now greater than Eleanor's.

"Can you tell me other things about what happened to you when you were a child?" I asked as he sat to rest on the bench. "When you were just eight. Did you know it was wrong?"

"Yes. I did know that." His voice was meek, submissive.

"It must have been the year Granny sent you and your brothers to live with that aunt? She was not a nice woman, Granny told me."

"No. She was—quite—quite unkind, really. She wouldn't let me have any milk and she'd give some to the older boys instead. I had to get up at five every morning and do all the chores while the others slept. I'd be so hungry."

"What a nightmare! She must have been demented. And you so young! But that other person who harmed you—in that other way. . . ."

"A neighbour."

"And he. . . ? Did he. . . ?" I suspected there was more than fondling.

"Yes."

"He penetrated you?"

"Yes." This was contrary to his first admission.

"You were so little. Poor Father. So very little."

I called Eleanor that night and told her his story. She agreed that it was all very sad. "But don't try to make excuses for him," she said. "You're not here in the world to absolve him. Who hasn't had trauma? There are no excuses. He had choices. So do you, Millicent."

Father and I were in the garden again the next day and I asked him about his victims—what their names were and where they now lived and whether he was in touch with them.

"You don't remember?"

He shook his head as he bent over to pull at weeds.

"Not anyone? What about the boys in the North?"

Father shook the earth from the roots of a thick clump. I thought he was ignoring me, but after a long pause, his voice between a whisper and a rasp, he said, "Rheimer."

"Was that his last name?"

"And Tobias."

"And they were? Tell me—were they Native children?"

"It was—it was all—a—a—terrible mistake. A terrible thing. . . ."

"What happened with Tobias?"

"He—he said he loved me. He forgave me. I had a letter. . . ."

"And you said there were others. How many others? You said there were thirty up north. But elsewhere—if you counted them all—the ones during your travels?" He was silent but I persisted. "Including everything—the fondling just one time, and whatever else. Were there—let's say—five hundred?" I knew it was an absurd figure. I expected he might laugh.

He started to go back towards the house. "No, not that many," he said. He reached the bottom of the front steps.

"Four hundred?"

His hands were holding the railing as he began to climb. I stood behind, ready to catch him in case he should fall. "A number have passed on."

"Were there four hundred?"

"No." He rested on the middle step as he said, "Three hundred, perhaps."

✧   ✧   ✧

It was like the time I got in the car and drove over the mountains and into the prairies, blindly seeking anonymity. I left him to climb the rest of the way alone. I ran up to my room and closed the door. I fell onto my bed, trembling. I reached over to the phone and dialled long-distance information, got the number of the diocesan headquarters and called. I told the secretary that I needed to see the bishop, the newly elected bishop, whom I'd never met. I told her it was urgent. The earliest I could see him was the following Wednesday. I said that wasn't soon enough. Then I ran back outside, passing Father in the hall. This time too I went without having packed, without thinking, without a single idea in my head about what I would say or how the bishop would react or what might happen. I drove into the evening and through the night, not trusting myself, not trusting anything. The Goddess was my conceit. The dream of mercy was a conceit. I cried into the darkness for Mother.

"You are such an impulsive child," I could hear her say. "So like your father."

"No, Mother," I wept. "I am not like my father."

I got lost entering the city. I asked at three gas stations for directions. I finally found a parking lot and sat watching the sun come up.

At nine o'clock, with my eyes covered in dark glasses, my face puffy from sleeplessness, I walked into the bishop's third-floor office. His secretary said he was in the middle of a meeting. He might be free at noon. I waited.

He was laughing when he came into the reception area. I was surprised by his youthful appearance and his casualness. Authority figures look so young to me these days. He was wearing a sport shirt and sweater. He was friendly, affable. "And what brings you here? What can I do for you?"

We sat in his large corner office, out of earshot of the receptionist. I started to speak. Then I stopped. He waited. I took the dark glasses off and covered my red eyes with my hands. "It's my father. I have to tell you about my father."

"Dr. Shelby. Ah yes. The founding saint of the Juniper Centres. A dear old gentleman. Is he all right?"

I waited until the uproar within me had subsided and then I began to speak. The words came at first haltingly, then in sudden spurts, small cloudbursts of words. His phone rang and he ignored it as the deluge broke within me in a long unstoppable telling. I brought forth the whole unmitigated story. The hard, hard stones of judgement, the dense and heavy weight that my frail love could not melt, were cast upwards into the blazing furnace of truth-telling.

When I was through, the bishop searched my face and said nothing. He looked stunned. It occurred to me that he might think I was insane.

"And none of the victims have come forward?"

"No. Not yet."

"Out of three hundred? Is that correct? I've never heard of anything like this."

"Do you not believe me?"

"It *is* hard to believe, Millicent." He was speaking softly in a flat monotone, his face expressionless.

"You can ask Peter Bowles at St. Chad's in Edmonton."

"I don't know him." He took a notebook from his desk and wrote down the name. He was shaking his head steadily. After a while, he said quietly, "What would Jesus do?"

I didn't know. What indeed would Jesus do—he, the Christ, the ancient one whose name today has become a curse? I imagined that, like the Goddess of Mercy, Jesus would stand with each of us. That is what love does. Was he not the one who stretched himself between heaven and earth without letting either go?

"Would he forgive? Are we to forgive endlessly, 'as to an idiot in the house'?" I asked.

The bishop was deep in thought for several more moments, his fingers moving back and forth across his forehead. Then, in a firm and deliberate voice, he said, "Millicent, you have to do whatever a daughter has to do. But I must do what a bishop has to do."

"And what is that?"

"The word that comes to my mind, as I think about your father, is tragedy. There are tragedies that are beyond our control. And beyond your control, Millicent. In a sense, this is out of your hands now, if I can help you by taking it out of your hands. . . ."

✦   ✦   ✦

I phoned Father from the hotel that night. I told him I'd gone to see the bishop. There was no response. I repeated myself.

"What was that, Millicent? The bishop?" His voice quivered. "The new bishop?"

"Yes. I had to tell him."

I hung up the phone. I didn't sleep again. The following afternoon I saw the bishop once more.

"If it were known—you understand this," he said. "If it were known that the church knew about this, and that we did nothing, the church would be liable."

I frowned. Liable? What did that word have to do with me? The bishop had taken off his pastoral hat of the day before and donned the hat of the administrator. "His victims must know that we stand with them and that we do not condone your father's behaviour. So if it was decided—you know that I must act on this information—that is, with your permission of course, and I assume I have your permission—and I'd need to consult with a few people first—"

"Consult? With?"

"We have a new policy in the diocese, a zero-tolerance policy. And a clear guide of disciplinary actions. We will need to have your story verified, of course, because all I have right now is your word. Then, if it was decided"—the bishop was speaking carefully, evenly. He was beginning to sound like a lawyer—"if it was felt that there should be deprivation of ministry or deposition from the exercise of ministry, all the metropolitans would have to be informed, all the clergy in the diocese. He would need his own legal counsel."

Whether it was the bishop's new tone of voice, or the mention of lawyers, or the spectre of a media spectacle, I felt a sudden chill. I clutched my throat in my mother's gesture of alarm, willing my hands to choke back a rising fear. "You're going to tell everyone? You're going to make this public? You mean all this—all this that I've told you in confidence—as in a confessional. . . ?" What could I possibly have been thinking in coming to see the bishop? I was just as mad as my father. Charlie and Mother were right. I never thought things through.

"Too much has been hidden for too long under the rubric of the confessional. And offences of this nature. . . . How many, Millicent?" He looked as if he seriously doubted the whole matter. Perhaps he was trying to shock me into withdrawing my outrageous allegations.

"You're going to—to expose Father and our family and—and unravel our lives for the sake of—for the sake of your institution?"

He breathed in deeply, looking up at the ceiling. Then he leaned forward. "We have to think of the victims first. The victims first. Justice demands that. We have to do whatever we can for them. And yes, I do think of the church—that she may face these matters forthrightly. Twenty years ago this would have been a private matter between the bishop and the priest. But not today. And of course, of course we must think of your family and your father. He has to be made to understand what he's done. He can't truly repent unless he first understands."

"But I was the one to bring this to you. No one else. And I'm not asking for public disgrace. How can it no longer be in my hands? I will have brought all this upon us with my own hands! My hands! Making this public will not help me. Or Jeffrey."

The panic within me was now full-blown. Was there not a promise when this journey began? I had walked in the way of Abraham, had I not? I had told the truth. Where was the safety now? "I've turned my father in," I said, my voice shaking. "He'll die. So will I." I knew that my words sounded calamitous and extreme and that I was trying to blackmail him into silence. I knew too that I was screaming as loudly as I could for help, for protection, for human mercy. "I will not live," I whispered, "as my father's betrayer."

The bishop looked sad and tired and old as he sat back in his chair. "The silence all these years, Millicent, that silent collusion, was a far, far greater betrayal."

CHAPTER TWENTY-SEVEN

"Have I indeed betrayed you, Father? Do you feel I have betrayed you?" I leaned forward, searching his face with my whispered question.

He seemed not to understand for a moment, then he shook his head. "No. You are not at fault, Millie dear. Not at all. I am the culprit." There was not a touch of anger or blame in his quiet reply. "The wrong was my doing." After a while, he added, "I can only hope that you can feel some ease now, some peace."

Whatever unimaginable crimes he has committed, I thought, there is still worth within him. A human being, simply by being human, retains dignity. And whatever all the world may say about Father, he is not a totally evil man. It is not in me to turn utterly against him.

As the days go by I am sitting with him while we wait for the action of the church. My loathing has been replaced by a terrible pity and sadness, and a shared dread. I do not know how Father is to come to understand what he has done, and how the boys and their families were affected and how their minds were scarred, unless the people themselves tell him.

In my dream this morning, all the trumpets had sounded and all the gates had opened wide and all the welcoming sounds of laughter filled the heavenly skies. It was then that the little ones, perpetually saddened, rose to block Father's view of paradise.

"It pleaseth Him that knoweth temptation," said the speaker of my dream, "not to continue with stories that are altogether lost."

"Oh Father," I cried, "you think you are lonely now. Consider the great loneliness yet to be unless the price is paid in understanding."

I tried to explain the dream to Father.

"Do you know, Millicent," he said, "I have begun to think that death must be like a very sound sleep. I find it a comforting thought."

"Your hope in eternity has become a hope for oblivion?"

"You might say that."

This afternoon, while Father was out, I went on my own search for more understanding. His study in this house is much smaller than the one in Juniper. Spilling out of bookshelves and in a cabinet and in boxes along the walls are piles of cards and correspondence—requests for prayer, for advice, intimate stories of pain and grief. I felt like a thief prowling through his private papers. "Thank you for your gift of a chicken farm. It will feed the village for years to come," said one beautifully handwritten letter from India. "Through knowing you I have touched the heart of love," said another. I opened his rolltop desk and saw a small alabaster figurine of Socrates in a crowded cubicle with little boxes of paper clips, rubber bands, stamps. Along the back were a few stacks of old correspondence neatly wrapped in red ribbons. Ah, the red ribbon that I saw on the fireplace hearth. One corner of the desk was empty, swept clean. This area must have held the papers and envelopes that I saw burning. Unfinished little stories going up in smoke.

Beside the silver-framed photograph of Granny Shelby on top of the desk was Mother's large-print Bible, and propped alongside it her old bookmark with a poem inscribed on it in Father's youthful hand. So often I had seen Mother caressing that bookmark, her clouded eyes no longer able to see the words.

The poem was signed, simply, "Your husband."

For Meredith

As to love and alteration
Let me say this:
Love alters that which
Love in constancy binds—
No, no, not binds, but
Beckons constantly, as to a
Prisoner Love would
Set free

For Love that is constant
Alters me, which is to say
I speak not of the human
But of the Divine, not of
The known, but of mystery.

My final word is Father's word. Mystery. It continues to be a mystery to me that Father, who spoke so much about the infinite power of Love, was a slave to such depravity. Perhaps the power of love is limited by the power of lies. Perhaps it is because he did not choose to walk in the way of truth that he was not sufficiently altered by the One who beckons constantly.

Although I am no closer to understanding Father or the ways of the universe, I do know where I, Millicent Shelby, stand. I am still the easily deluded woman I have always been, but I have faced the truth, I have spoken the truth, I have earned my passage.

As the bishop and the lawyers and the committee meet to contemplate their procedures against Father, I am ready. We are to stand together, he and I, under the harsh and merciless light of the newspaper moon. It is not so much that I choose to be with him or against him, or to be with or against the world, but that the Goddess beckons through the fire towards life. While all this that I have most dreaded is upon us and the flames of loathing rise, this is the grace that is granted: the Presence of Mercy, the promise of Abundance. The journey will lead into the abundant way.

Ultimately, my father's soul is not mine to defend or condemn, to save or to slay. It is the Great Mother who birthed us all, who holds to her breast the child who at best will go often astray. With weeping and mourning she watches as we venture on our wayward wandering. She awaits us all as our envoy and angel in the midst of the consuming flames. There in the red-hot lava of her tears, all judgement must be dissembled and dissolved.

✧   ✧   ✧

And now, to those who seek the merciful way, there is granted this sure knowledge: that the seeds of mercy are planted in the human condition, within each of us, between and among and towards us all, men, women, children, majorities, minorities— all people who know betrayal and enmity. We are to water with our tears the hidden seeds lying dormant in the spirals of our hearts, till they grow and flower and spread truth and healing over us. Thus shall we inherit the earth.

PART THREE

To every story there is an after-story, and to every life an afterwards. Beyond each punctuation point, each period, are further questings and more bends in the road ahead than we can imagine.

It is five years now since Father died.

In these, my after-father years, I have found a new world, dense and sweet as honey and friendship. Life is dramatically different these days, but the mystery of Father remains. I did not understand him before and understand him no better today. The thief who came in the night, dressed in black, was darkness camouflaged in darkness. But he was also carried on the wings of a blue-veined light.

It is all so much more than my efforts to describe can manage. I faced the stone-throwers, silent and vocal—those who blamed me for inaction, those who found me guilty by association, those who could not abide any closeness to me and who felt safer by erecting walls to shut me out. I survived it all.

I continue to survive. If I could discover the precise steps to my new and growing freedom, I might try to show the way. I could hold up a placard and shout, "This way! This way!" But I can hardly fathom, let alone explain, the change. New friends here at the Ontario Juniper Centre comment on my equanimity, and I say, "It hasn't always been so." I have tried a few times to speak of my journey but ended up sounding idiotic or, I thought, deranged or, even worse, false. One person concluded that the Goddess of Mercy was "a magnificent fiction, but still just a fiction." Perhaps that is so. Perhaps it is not. If our truths, in the end, are what we are compelled to believe from the evidence at hand, then love, for me, is the way, the truth and the life. I know no other hope. And all I can do is declare these facts: once I was weak, once my body was wretched and ill, once I was a woman in flight; now I am well. I am more than well. This is all that I have been given to know. But I keep learning, as the journey continues, that there are deeper untransformed truths waiting to come to the light.

The seed, it seems to me, is more powerful than the flower in bloom; the stories that are hidden from us, more powerful than the ones we tell.

❖   ❖   ❖

I waken this morning to the sounds of birdsong and laughter, the Canada bird singing, its patriotic "Oh Ca—na—na—na—na—na" announcing "the true north, strong and free." Outside in the tent, not far from my open window, I can hear the children's rollicking shouts. The lone bird, clear and unperturbed, maintains its piercing two-tone call.

Elsewhere inside this rambling old Juniper Camp lodge, the whoosh and gurgle of plumbing signals a morning stumbling awake. It's going to be a busy week. Registration for the day camp begins at two o'clock tomorrow. The familiar comings and goings of my childhood, the full and flowing music-filled days are back once more. I am happy in this. The staff's do-it-yourself breakfast is in an hour, at eight in the screened porch of the lodge overlooking the lake. We'll all have a picnic lunch later at the beach. Yesterday, Kate phoned at noon to say she'd be coming for a month this fall. I can hardly wait.

I first met Kate Middleton, Archdeacon Kate Middleton, in Ragland, about six years ago, a little over two months after my frantic flight to see the bishop. Father and I had been expecting we knew not what—a letter, a summons—some sort of communication. Yet week after week nothing was happening. I was beginning to feel that things might continue as they always had. After all, the church had known years before. Then there were two long-distance calls—one from the church, one from the press. The first was expected; the second was not.

I was tidying the living room when the first call came. Long distance. A prim-sounding voice asked for Canon Shelby.

"He's resting," I said. "I'm sorry. Is there a message?"

"Archdeacon Middleton," the diocesan secretary said crisply, "is driving to the coast and expects to be through Ragland the week of the twelfth. Would Tuesday be possible?"

Promptly at two o'clock on the appointed day, there was a rather tentative knock. I had imagined a male cleric, tall perhaps, thin and austere, and was surprised when I opened the door. The archdeacon was a woman, middle-aged, more stocky than plump, round glasses, her white dog-collar stark and official against her navy blue. She stood, hands together, as Father, his shoes polished, wearing his second-best grey-green suit, shuffled into the living room to meet his interrogator.

"Archdeacon Middleton, this is my father." Her nod was, I thought, curt.

Father eased himself onto the edge of his armchair. He did not lean back. Neither did she, as she sat opposite him on the couch, her back straight. If Father was surprised to see a woman archdeacon, he did not let on. His eyes were wide, childlike. Whether by intent or not, trust and innocence were declared in his open gaze. After a brief moment of small talk— the view of the mountains, the plants in the sunroom that she could see if she turned—she directed the conversation to other topics. She knew Eleanor, and had met her recently again in Calgary at a conference on reconciliation. In her childhood, she'd often heard "Shelby Selects."

"You're a living legend, Canon Shelby. You have many admirers." Father shifted uncomfortably and looked down at the carpet.

We knew why she had come. If Mother were present, she'd be saying as she so often did, "Cling to God, Barnabas. Life can be so punishing—so cruel. But that's when we must cling the hardest. Cling as if your life depended on it."

Archdeacon Middleton, mercifully, was not an imposing figure. Her efforts to put us at ease were not wasted. I offered her tea. Perhaps it was her lopsided homey smile, or the ordinariness of teacups, milk and sugar—or perhaps it was the sun on my arm and Boots batting a dustball at my feet—that made me begin to feel almost relaxed. No chilling staccato of violins to signal anything sinister.

"I am here—you know that I have come to talk with you about—your problem." She was quietly earnest. She asked, as I had, about his childhood.

Father responded in one-word sentences, his head bowed.

"You were accosted by the neighbour, you say, just once?" She was frowning as she took out a notepad. It seemed impossible that a single childhood sexual trauma could account for a lifetime's perversion. She shuffled through what looked like several pages of notes. I wondered how much the bishop had conveyed to her.

"We understand so little," she said. "Perhaps you could help us, Canon Shelby."

Father could not help. He could not say the words. It was as if that part of him that remained in civil company could not bridge the gap. Nor could I. The pauses were long as she waited patiently for Father to speak. Had he been sexually oriented towards children all his life?

I could not tell what the intention was for the visit, and what she had been sent to do. It occurred to me briefly, as she glanced back and forth through her notes, that it might be my sanity that was on trial, and that she had come to verify my talk with the bishop. But the thought passed. Clearly, she was trying to understand as much as she could. Beneath her quiet questioning, I could not detect any emotion—neither loathing nor pity. She could have been asking the time of day.

"How do you think of your sexuality—if you, say, compare it. . . ?"

I doubted that Father ever thought of himself as so different from others. One's sexuality was a private matter after all, was it not? People did not talk about such things.

She did not press for more than he could say. She turned to me and her voice was kind as she asked, "You must have thought about all this so much, Millicent. How do you see...?"

"How do I see the contradictions?"

"Yes. The contradictions, if you like. How do you see your father?"

"I—yes, I have thought about it—and my guess is that— Father, that—that you're still—in so many ways—still just eight years old. You're still locked in that first trauma. Hooked by it."

"Hooked?" she asked.

"Yes," I said, nodding. "Hooked. I think that's the word." There was something so genuinely childlike in Father. He was trusting, excitable, contagiously enthusiastic and so whole-hearted. I'd often thought of him as a child in a man's body, a Peter Pan, a boy who never grew up and who spent his lifetime battling Captain Hook in his own never-never land with other lost boys. Could this be Father's story, I wondered aloud— Peter Pan hooked in Captain Hook's embrace, attempting to reconcile an irreconcilable experience?

"You're suggesting that Peter Pan is Captain Hook? And Captain Hook is Peter Pan?" Kate Middleton looked at me quizzically, and at Father, who appeared to be as puzzled as she.

"I—I think I'm saying something like that."

She considered this for a moment, then shook her head slightly and said, "But that's not the story for every lost boy, is it?"

This was Eleanor's point over and over again. "Not all children who are molested become molesters," she'd said. This was the chorus sung in unison by the lawmakers, the justice seekers.

The weight of the argument was a stone in my chest. I would never be able to expel it, however deeply and often I might sigh. It remained undeniable. We are creatures of choice. Where one person sees pearls, another sees pellets of dung, as Father himself used to say. Not all lost boys would choose to become Captain Hooks.

I had spent a lifetime looking for excuses. I was still looking. It had become a way of being.

Father was searching our faces, his eyes beseeching.

Kate Middleton put her notepad and pen away, then quietly, as if to herself, she asked, "In your private devotions, Canon Shelby . . . where do you suppose . . . where was God?"

Father, hands folded like a schoolboy's, his brow arched in perplexity, lifted his gaze beyond Kate's prayerful face, out past the window, beyond the walls, beyond the hills.

Where was God?

This one great timeless question. Where, for my father, where, for the children, where, for the victims of everyday crimes and crimes unimaginably horrible, was God? And where, today, for the countless children of Abraham who war with each other in rivalry and rage—Christians—Protestants, Catholics—Muslims—Jews—where for the children of poverty and the criminals of wealth, where for the unfeeling hordes of us and the unseen vast legions of the world's victims, where today in the great unforgiven and unforgiving world is God?

In the seeking where there is no finding, in the knocking where no door opens, in the absence where the cry for love is met by betrayal and in that great terrible silence filled with a suffering that knows no solace, where is God? Where are You, my God, my Goddess, at such times, in such places? Where, in the mystery of the absence of love, are You?

Merciful and Abundant One, I know You as the Friend, hidden but not absent, who walks steadfastly with us through the conundrums and mazes and terrors of our unknowing, and through the porous walls between worlds. You lead us as surely as the North Star guides the sailors of the seas, beyond our time-heavy travel to the places where You are. You carry us there, You carry me here, now, to the moving of Your steady, still, wonderful light, Your luminous, warm, becoming everywhere light. You are where love is, as it resides even within our creaturely crookedness and our so strange and bent encountering and in our recognition of our hunger for You. You cry that impossible cry within us that the ancient psalmist cried.

"My God, my God, why hast Thou forsaken me?"

Merciful One, You know our utter despair. That cry anchored in the depths of the human heart forms the structure of the bridge between us and You. At the heart of the impossible, in the doorways that lead nowhere, in our incomprehension and in the extremity of our abandonment, You are. In all that is lost, in all that suffers, You are. In the silence more than in the speaking, in our dread and our weeping, You are. Beyond what I could have dreamed possible, You are.

Beloved Friend, I know You in the love that shone through my wretched father's life more than in Charlie's or Eleanor's righteousness and judgements. I know You better in the sinner than the saint. I glimpse You on the city streets where the homeless ones lie, and in the dying woods and streams I know You. And more dearly, more nearly, have I known You in my plea for mercy than in the great good call for justice. I know You in the world's many wondrous stories of compassion as I know You in the One who came as Love and who died, forgiving and forsaken and broken. In all the hoping, praying, dreaming, trusting places where light and shadow struggle, You are. And now in this my every-morning new day, as on that afternoon six years ago when Father and Kate Middleton and I searched the skies asking where You were, the question bearing no judgement, the silence filled with trust. You were there. You are here.

Kate Middleton's face was peaceful as she acknowledged the healing balm within the meditative listening that greeted her question.

In response to my own question about her inner journey, she tried, as I have also tried since, to explain, stumbling over her words and laughing at the failure of this clumsy tool we call language.

"At least start by calling me Kate," she said as I continued to address her formally as Archdeacon Middleton. She spoke of the primacy of friendship in her life—her friendship with the Source of friendship, her radical friendships with the demonized persons of the day, "who are no more demons than I am." Friendship, for her, was the most necessary work of our day—not the easy act of engaging with the like-minded, but the arduous, world-altering labour of befriending the enemy.

"And this you take to be an archdeacon's task? This is your profession?"

She laughed at the term "professional friendship," calling it an oxymoron.

Father, his eyes closed, leaned back in his armchair as the conversation flowed around him.

"How do you manage to see friends where others see demons?" I asked.

"You've heard the phrase 'They became what they beheld'?"
I had.

"I think we behold what we are," she said. "We say, 'They this. They that. They. They devour. They are monsters.' And all that venting, all that rage, reflects ourselves. We deflect the horror of what we collectively are doing. Devouring the planet. Devouring the children. Devouring the future."

"We consume because we are consumed? We are consumed by the need to consume?"

"Yes. Yes. But we also love because we are loved."

I didn't know if Father was listening or understanding. He almost seemed to be falling asleep. The Comforter was present to me in Kate Middleton's thoughtful presence. But how the justice-seeking, zero-tolerance church intended to deal with Father, I did not know.

It was as she was preparing to leave that I finally asked, "Could you tell me what we might expect from the church? Father and I?"

She rummaged through her purse for a somewhat worn business card. "Millicent, you must feel free to call me at any time." She wrote her home phone number on the back of the card and handed it to me. "Any time at all." Then, looking from me to Father, who was struggling to stand, and back to me again, she assured us that there would be no public flogging, no tar and feathers, no dragging through the streets—at least, not by the church. A letter would go out to the bishops. We would get a copy. His licence would be revoked.

I walked down the front steps with her to her car. Across the street, an elderly woman from the choir at St. John's glanced over at us. She stopped and waved.

"Lovely day," she called cheerfully. "How is your father, Millicent?"

"Oh, he's all right," I called back a little weakly. "Tired these days, though."

"We miss him in church. Will you tell him?" She glanced curiously at Kate Middleton, a stranger in a clerical collar, who nodded and smiled her lopsided smile. Our friendly, airy gestures, my nonchalant wave, were keeping the secret securely locked away. There would be no introductions today. Should the imps break loose and leap towards the nice, trusting people of St. John's, should the mad mobs get a whiff of the scandal, the sky would turn red with blood.

As she crossed the street towards us, I shrank back. All that was needed was one report. "She's going to find out, isn't she," I whispered. "The whole town will know."

Kate Middleton put a firm hand on my shoulder. "Stand tall, Millicent," she whispered back. "Hold your head up. You hold your head up high."

CHAPTER TWENTY-NINE

I didn't know it that day, but the seeds of friendship firmly planted would grow over time into a flowering, sheltering tree.

"You hold your head up, Millicent." I found myself repeating her words like a mantra. At times the parting whisper would take on the tones of a biblical chant. "Lift up your heads, O ye gates; and be ye lift up, ye everlasting doors. . . ."

Kate did not wait for me to call her. She rang before the week was up. She and Eleanor and I talked on a three-way connection for over an hour.

I told them that Father, in his confusion, was starting to call me Meredith from time to time.

"You have to get away from there, Mills," Eleanor said. "I keep telling you. Come and stay in Cha Cha's old room."

Theatrical Cha Cha, with her black-lined Cleopatra eyes and eyelashes thick as spiders' legs, had moved out years earlier in an orgy of rebellion and was now living a raucous life as an oversized model. The last time I'd seen Cha Cha's room, the walls had still been painted shiny cinnamon and black.

I knew it was unhealthy to stay with Father, but I could not see myself blown about in the volatile Eleanor–Charlie winds. At mealtimes, in the hallways, I'd been so often trapped in their unpredictable arguments. Then, almost on cue, they'd turn and I'd become Charlie's avenue of rage. It was habitual, Charlie and I in our old rut and Charlie saying things like "What goes on in that rattletrap of a brain of yours?" Or "The problem with a blabbermouth is a blabbermouth." And always, with a curl of the lip, the "You and Father" comments.

I stayed at home. I made Father's meals and left them for him. I cleaned up when he went back to his room. I lived within a dailiness that sometimes felt like normalcy. But there were other moments—moments that I still regret—when I was so sick of Father, literally sick, when the revulsion was so overwhelming, that my mind and body could not contain it. Once, when he'd been unwell and unable to get out of bed, I had left some burnt toast for him—cold and inedible—and that was supper. He did say, feebly, one night, "Perhaps, Millie dear, we should consider my placement in—in—the convalescent home?"

There were forty-seven people ahead of him on the waiting list at Ragland Lodge. In the meantime, I had a lifeline system installed so that I could be away more often. He was to wear a chain necklace with an oval button at all times. "If anything happens when I'm not home," I told him, "press the button and a phone call will go out to the neighbours."

"A phone call, did you say? From that?" He frowned at the new loudspeaker box on the table by his bed.

"A call first goes to Boston. It's absurd, I know. We used to have a local service."

Father looked at the device without comprehension.

Kate's friendship in those trying days was a pure gift. We were both, she said, seekers of the light, hungry for the light. I saw her at first as a representative of the church, a church that housed both healing and harm. But the more we travelled the truth-strewn path, and the more nakedly we walked, the further her role within the institution receded. Her own private demon was a recurring depression.

I can say this: that the friendship of prayer is deeply transformative. The wounded mind refocusses. When our confidence in our friendship faltered, our confidence in our Friend would not. What began for me as an occasional silver lining around storm clouds has become a tenacious light surrounding, challenging, even dispelling the raging dark.

It was several months after Kate's first visit that the phone call came from a reporter, signalling a new time of trial. My private nightmares were about to leap through the trap door and out into the public world of print.

"Miss Shelby? I'm from *The Examiner*." The husky voice on the phone was a sudden gust of sleet.

My stammering sounded shrill. "I'm sorry—he—he's—not well. He can't come to the phone." This was true. Father was deteriorating, physically and otherwise. One bad flu lingered and developed into pneumonia. More than once he'd fallen. He was spending less time at his desk and more in bed. A young couple from St. John's had begun to bring over the week's service sheets since Father had stopped going to church. Some mornings I would find him kneeling by his bed, eyes closed, face to heaven, fingers pressed tightly together. Once I saw him clasping Mother's Bible to his lips, his praying face flooded with tears.

"When should I call back?"

"I'm sorry. He's not taking calls."

But she did call again, and again I replied that Father was unwell. Then, about a week later, she arrived, a young fit-looking woman with a bulky black bag and camera over her shoulder.

I did not let her in. I called both Kate and Eleanor and we agreed that I should grant no interviews with Father to anyone. I was not going to answer the phone any more. If either of them should call, they could leave word on the answering machine. Courageous lovers of the light though they both were, they understood the appeal of the shadows.

The reporter, Jacqueline Addison, was the most undeterred person I've ever met. She left a long message saying she was writing an article on The Juniper Band Its, a "scrub and tub" band that had been spawned years ago at the Juniper Centre. "I couldn't complete my piece without their famous mentor."

When I answered the door the next day, she was there with a half-dozen roses, saying she hoped he was feeling better. I smiled wanly and thanked her but, again, did not invite her in.

Then on Wednesday morning, the following week, I returned from the post office and stores to find her in the living room with Father, unshaven, in his bathrobe. She had a tape recorder running on the coffee table and was in full interview mode. I almost dropped the bag of groceries in my panic.

"Peter Bowles?" I heard Father ask as I closed the door. His face was ashen. This was clearly not an interview about The Band Its, or, if so, there was more to the article than music.

"Father, you should be in bed." I didn't acknowledge her.

She stood and extended her hand to me, leaving the tape recorder running.

"Father is not well," I said as I took his arm in my attempt to get him to his feet. As I did so, she jumped to his other side.

"No, no. We'll manage." She must think she's his hired nurse, I thought, as she ignored me and assisted his wobbly walk to his embarrassingly smelly and messy room. Like Mother, he was now quite incontinent, and his cloudy urine sat in its turquoise-coloured container, like a bent plastic milk-bottle vase, on top of his table. Hurriedly I removed it, thinking that the whole house probably reeked of urine.

Her reporter's eyes took in the evidence from Father's crowded study, library, bedroom, the wardrobe door open, the coat hooks hung with old belts and suspenders that he hadn't used in years, the walls covered in photographs—skim skim— an ornate banner from India, several citations. The invader was invading the den of the invader.

Father lay in his bed clutching the afghan up to his chin, his right hand shaking steadily as I ushered Jacqueline Addison out of the room and back to the still-running tape recorder.

"You're interested in more than The Band Its."

She shrugged. "They're well named, don't you think?"

I pointed to the tape recorder. "Would you please. . . ."

As she pressed the button and the tiny click brought me one tiny step back from a looming brink, I asked, "Peter Bowles?"

"Yes."

"He spoke with you?"

"Off the record."

"And you came here to. . . ."

She studied my face, then asked abruptly, "How do you stay with him?"

I studied her back and said nothing. How much did she know?

"How do you live with a person who has no conscience?" she persisted.

The gulf between her experience of life and mine was, I thought, unbridgeable. A complete abyss.

"I believe his—his conscience is—is. . . ." I couldn't think of any way to convey his humanity to her. I imagined that, in her mind, the filthy old pervert quivering in the other room was altogether subhuman. Her task, her God-given task for all I knew, was to sweep the streets clean of him and his obscene stench. My grey-shaded portrait of a sinner could have no place in her gallery of sharp black and white clarity.

I was floundering my way through her unrelenting questions when we both heard a loud thud from Father's room.

"What was that?" We rushed to find Father, flat on his face and still as a fallen log, on the floor beside his desk.

CHAPTER THIRTY

Breath breath breath breath. . . .

"Could it have been caused by stress?" I asked the doctor.

"It's possible. Anything's possible."

Father's eyes were closed in a frown. His head was propped up and his hospital bed was rolled up in a reclining position. Tubes were in his nostrils and another was on his hand.

I cupped my mouth to his ear. "Father, it's Millicent."

He groaned one long, last agonizing attempt at speech. It ended in a final sound of utter weariness as his head, a heavy weight on his neck, rolled across the pillow. And then it lay still. A stone.

"Can you hear me, Father?"

No answer. No sound ever again.

I moistened the gauze in a tray of water and wiped his closed eyelids.

"Is he in pain?" I asked the doctor the next day.

"We don't know. With such a massive stroke—we don't know."

Father struggling to breathe, phlegm in throat, in lungs, the spirit riding riding above the yellow hospital sheets and the slow drip drip through plastic tubing into the back of his right hand.

Eleanor and Charlie, on tour in France, did not feel compelled to return. "He could be like that for months," Eleanor said.

"No. I know it won't be long. I know."

She said they'd discuss it. In the end they chose their tour. They chose life.

"We have to take care of ourselves," Eleanor said. "You don't understand. . . ."

"Mills, you don't understand," Charlie shouted into the mouthpiece, echoing Eleanor just the way he used to echo Mother.

"You're right, Charlie," I shouted back. "I don't understand. I'm like Father. He didn't understand either. You're the only one who understands. You and Eleanor. You. . . ."

They hung up.

The following day, while I was at the hospital, Eleanor called back and left a message. "It's harder for Charlie, Millicent. It's much harder for him. You've no idea."

When I called the hotel, I was told they'd checked out. I thought they might call the next day and stayed at home for the phone. It didn't ring.

I didn't know what form of consciousness remained for Father. I didn't know how long things would last. I summoned St. Michael and all his angels to do battle across the field of my mind. I called for the forces of human compassion to stand in their glory, fine and clear, strong as fire, vast as ocean, red and glowing as sea and sunset, flaming forth from every bud and bush and shrub on the battlefield. Called upon our limitless connectedness one to another, our limitless capacity to encompass our many desolations. Called upon the wisdom beyond my knowing. "Assist this man," I prayed, "even now, to the right road, the right direction, the right thought."

The phlegm wormed its way down the side of his mouth. I put the suction tube there to draw it, whitish-grey slime, down the piping, gurgling into the plastic jug on the wall, where it sat like sludge.

Like sludge I too sat, in my own puddle of slime, my eagerness for his departure mixed with regret. Regret that we had not said goodbye. Regret that the last days were not ones of kindness. Regret, the currency of poverty.

I waited by his hospital bed. He seemed to be at peace. How could one tell?

"I'm ready for you to go, Father," I whispered. "Charlie and I are both ready. Any time you want to go is all right. Are you still eager to stay?"

For days, there was no change. "Peaceful, isn't he," the priest from St. John's said when he dropped by. "He's a good man, your father."

"He's dying," I said.

Father's left leg jerked as I said this. One motion. I wondered then whether he was conscious and trying to communicate that he was still alive, that he could hear, that he wasn't ready to die.

"What are the chances of his recovery?" I asked the doctor on his rounds that afternoon.

He shook his head. "In cases like this—at his age—if he does survive, he'll simply vegetate."

"He'd wanted to go suddenly."

"It was sudden for him," the doctor said.

I indicated the needle in his hand. "And that. . . ?"

"It's up to you."

"What would you do?"

"If it were me—I wouldn't want to linger. Not like that."

"No."

We agreed. I learned later that one of the parishioners, a former nurse, had visited and criticized my decision. She had known of other stroke victims who had been able to recover.

There were five more days of waiting. Five long days. Parishioners dropped by with cards and flowers. A beautiful young woman with a guitar arrived from out of town one afternoon. "He's been a hero of mine for years," she told me. There was a tear in Father's eye as her lilting sweet voice sang English folk songs.

On another day, I told him again of my dream. "Father, it's understanding. . . .You have to have understanding. Even now. And afterwards. Can you understand what I'm trying to say? It's after you hear all the stories, after that, after you under-stand, and the boys have all had their say—that's when heaven opens its doors. At least, that's what my dream said. Father, can you hear me?" I could not tell. His brow was furrowed as I was speaking, as if in pain.

Nurses came by to check his pulse, to wash his inert body, his arms and legs no longer volitional, the lump of his form rolled onto his side. I turned my eyes away from his nakedness.

In the TV lounge, a thin old man, his blue hospital gown open at the back, was standing, facing but not watching the television. There was a story of a bear cub at a zoo. Nine months old. It had been found lost in the Arctic, orphaned. Its paws held its head.

Lostness.

Infants. Mute. Lonely beyond description in concrete cages.

That night when I got home, there was a message. Eleanor had called. They were on their way to Morocco. Cha Cha had called them. The story was on page four of *The Examiner*. "Founder of Juniper Centres Accused of Abuse."

"She's so upset, Millicent." I could hear the TV blaring in the background.

I lay exhausted and sleepless on the couch. The next day was Saturday. Father's breathing was rapid and laboured. The nurse said it wouldn't be long. I was thinking I should stay. I could stay. I could line up the chairs and form a bed and rest and watch over him through the night. But I didn't.

In the early, still dark morning I was in a stupor, struggling in a dream, when I woke with a start, my heart pounding. A moment later, the phone by my bed rang.

"Miss Shelby, it's the night nurse calling."

Thanksgiving Sunday. Five-fifteen a.m.

I rose numbly, drove to the hospital, walked quickly quickly through the quiet corridors to his room. Two strangers in white were at his side.

I watched his body being tied and wrapped with white string and white plastic and I thought of Thanksgiving turkeys being trussed for roasting. An irreverent thought. I touched his cheek. Cold. Reached my arm down his back. Still warm. The two strangers, doing their job, waited for me. I didn't say the words out loud, but I mouthed them. "Goodbye, Father." When they turned him on his side, his body was stiff. So dead.

I walked with them as they wheeled him away. Down the elevator to a cold room. In the hall outside the closed door, I folded my hands together, my fingertips covering my mouth as I whispered old songs from "Shelby Selects" so softly that no one could hear.

"Godspeed, Father," I said in my mind. "Thanksgiving Sunday is a good day. You picked a good day to go."

CHAPTER THIRTY-ONE

Father was buried almost a week later, on a blustery Friday the thirteenth.

I had delayed the day hoping Eleanor and Charlie might come, but in the end it was just two of us in the funeral chapel, saying our quiet farewells. No sidespersons ushering in lines of mourners. No eulogies. Kate and I stood facing the coffin, a simple unadorned box. I pictured Eleanor and Charlie with us, each standing at a corner, a little rectangular vigil. And I thought of the picture in my childhood bedroom of four angels around the bed of a sleeping child.

Four corners to my bed, four angels round my head,
One to watch and two to pray, and one to keep all fear away.

I wept for the child, Charles Barnabas, Granny Shelby's genius baby reading a newspaper to astonished passengers on board a ship. I wept for that innocent and wondrous little boy, a hope-shaped light trapped within a criminal's life.

Father's old trumpet rested on top of the closed coffin, beside a small cluster of roses from the garden and a cutting from the night-blooming cereus. I picked it up, muted it, opened a window and played "Taps" softly and slowly into the passing traffic.

Day is done
Gone the sun
From the hills
From the lakes
From the sky. . . .

We drove to the cemetery in the customary limousine, with the men from the funeral home, and watched as the plain wooden box was lowered mechanically to his grave beside Mother's. Flesh and bone to dust and stone.

✧   ✧   ✧

Looking back these years later, I can see with the eyes in the back of my skull that, as in fairy tales and legends, so in life— the time of the test is a fire that fixes the faith. Day by hour by moment, the Merciful One was present, even as I stood under the lurid glow of *The Examiner*'s glare.

Father, who was in a coma when the headlines hit, never had to face the public humiliation. That was left to the rest of us.

The streets of Ragland turned overnight to quicksand. The shopkeeper, who used to deliver our groceries, didn't know what to say and averted his eyes when I dropped by to pay the monthly bill. He whispered to his wife, who awkwardly accepted my cheque, then they both hastily turned to another customer. One of the high school teachers who would often stop to chat crossed the street to avoid me, and resolutely looked away. The neighbour on the next block whose two cherubic little girls I would often watch playing shepherded them towards the house when she saw me coming down the street. I walked past as quickly as I could. When I turned the corner, I glanced back and found her still staring after me, eyes fearful and wide.

"Lift up, oh lift up your head, Millicent," I said to myself. But I couldn't.

The Alberta Juniper Centre's silence was a thick concrete wall when I enquired, more than once, if they would like Father's archival material. Charlie and Eleanor too wanted nothing, nothing, nothing at all from the house. "Burn the stuff. Do anything you want. Just don't bug us," Charlie said. Cha Cha at first wanted the family silver, some albums and the gifts that had never been used. Thank heavens, I thought. But she changed her mind. The fallout of *The Examiner*'s story was affecting more than their social calendars. Cha Cha lost her job and moved back home. In one raving phone call she screamed at me. It was all my fault. I had ruined their lives.

"Dad says you're just as selfish and pig-headed and sick as Grandad. You were wrong to be on his side. It's so sick. You make me so sick I could puke. You had no business speaking to that reporter."

"Cha Cha, I didn't tell her. . . ."

"Don't call here. Don't ever call here again. We've got nothing to do with you or your sickening old filthy old disgusting. . . ." I could hear Eleanor in the background. And then she hung up. Eleanor phoned back to say that, for now, it was better if I didn't phone.

I called Kate. I wept. We prayed. She told me all this was typical. Families of the demonized devour one another. I should look away. I tried. But I couldn't bear it. I reached out more than once.

"You think the whole world revolves around you, Mills? Get a life. Leave us alone!" The words from my brother hit me in the face like lye.

Over time, I have had so many body blows from Father's hidden past that I know by now I am in the ring for life. But I am not alone in my corner. My coach is the great Shadow Boxer, who takes the punches with me. More than once I've been knocked out by passing remarks. "I always thought you weren't normal. You couldn't be normal living with somebody like that." People, even strangers, have phoned, they've sent e-mails. "It's not true, is it? It can't be true." I've run into a few of his victims by chance—once at a wedding, once in a café, once in the middle of the road as we were walking in opposite directions. I've heard from almost a dozen people. I wonder about the hundreds of others. What I've learned is that the story of an abuser is not a story of an individual. It's a story of a web.

About two weeks after the article by Jacqueline Addison, an old classmate from Juniper High, now living in Regina, called to tell me that her daughter needed to talk. "Kelly Ann put two and two together," she said.

Kelly Ann's high tiny voice was that of a child. "I didn't believe it. I would never, never, have believed. My sister told me when Brad and I got engaged. But I said she was just jealous. Brad would never do anything like that."

"Like what?"

"Like take her into the woods."

"Was that so bad?"

"But she was six. He was sixteen."

"Oh."

Kelly Ann had lived in denial. She'd seen the evidence and dismissed it—the locked bathroom door, the baby's reddened genital area. She'd seen Brad with his hands jiggling under Jilly's blanket. He'd said, "I was just seeing if she was wetting herself." She had begun to wonder about her sister's story for the first time.

The day after her mother showed her the article, she began questioning Brad. He was not a talker. He denied everything at first. Then the story, only part of the story, emerged. Something had happened with Father. Once? Twice? Often? He wouldn't say. She started to watch him closely. He refused to go for therapy.

"I can't believe anything he says. Anything. I can't leave him in the house with Jilly. It's crazy. I'm going crazy. Should I get a divorce? Do I want a divorce? The priest says I can't get a divorce anyway. God doesn't allow it. I'm just going crazy."

"Oh, Kelly Ann. There are other priests."

She called several times over the following days. She saw the Lutheran minister who encouraged her to see a lawyer. Brad claimed she was making everything up. He said he was going to move out and sue for custody. Over the phone I held Kelly Ann's hand. "We're going to come out of this, Kelly Ann," I told her. "He can't take Jilly. I'll come if it will help. I'll testify."

Brad was just one of Father's many boys. Three others phoned, and one came to visit to tell me of his relief when the story was out. As young boys they had tried to hide from him, one had tried to protect a younger brother. None of them had told their parents. One woman I could hardly remember called to say that her brother would kill her if he knew she was speaking to me, so deep was his rage.

"If you knew what the creep was up to, why didn't you turn him in? What's wrong with you? What's wrong with your whole family?"

I listened to her and my first impulse was to run away somewhere, anywhere. I wanted to hang up the phone, get an unlisted number. I wanted to tell her it wasn't my fault. But as her choking anger turned to tears, I found myself condemning my complicity, the cowardice of silence. How could I have been so blind? How could I not have seen her brother, her family?

"What can I—is there anything I can do? Anything?" My question was to the Great Healer as much as to her.

The bitterness exploded in my ear. "Nothing. There's not a damn thing you can do. Your family wrecked my family and you can live with that. You can eat shit is what you can do. You can go to hell!"

"I'm so—I am so sorry," I whispered.

"You think just because you say you're sorry that makes everything all right?"

"No—no. Of course it doesn't." Words were so cheap, I thought. Nothing I could say would help. If Father had been publicly hounded, sent to jail, castrated in public, if he had suffered and she had been able to see the suffering, that might have eased her pain. Was it now left to me, to Charlie, to carry that load?

There is a time to speak and a time not to speak. This was a time when neither speech nor silence would suffice.

When I finally hung up the phone, I was too full of weeping to do anything except put my head on the desk and heave with sobs. The tidal wave of pain was never going to end. Where in all the world was a happier place? I called Kate, but she was out. Eventually I crawled into bed, fully clothed, too tired to undress.

Somewhere in the night, Mercy attended me. In the morning I woke with the old Beatles' song "Let It Be" running through my mind. "Let It Be." Though I was branded the enemy, even my accusers were likewise branded. Humanity was replete with crimes—crimes of leaders, of ancestors, crimes in the name of God, crimes of action and countless crimes of inaction. We were all members of tribes and nations and families, none of which could claim either pure innocence or pure guilt.

I prayed through the following days that Father's victims and their families would find the help they needed, would find a measure of relief and ease. I prayed to the Maker of Hope, whose rainlight arcs towards heaven and bows again to earth in that gentle greeting of colour and light, "Send hope. Rain down hope, oh Author of hope. Send hope." I clung to Kate. I clung to Eleanor.

Then late one Saturday night Cha Cha called and her voice was subdued. "Auntie, I'm really worried about you. You've got to go and see a doctor."

"A what?"

"Mom just told me about Jeffrey. Why didn't you call the police? It's unbelievable, Aunt Mills. Unbelievable! Don't you know there's something really wrong with this picture? Didn't you care about your own child? What if he'd killed Jeff?"

"I'd do anything for Jeffrey, Cha Cha. But putting Grandad in jail—that wouldn't have helped Jeff at all. Not at all."

"But you know why Grandad got away with it, don't you. It's because you protected him. You put the gun in his filthy hand and you said, "Okay, Daddy darling, go and kill my little baby. . . .""

"Cha Cha, I can't hear this."

"No. That's what Mom and Dad both told me. You can't face the truth. And you know what? Here's something else you can chew on. Either you go and get help for yourself, or you don't ever ever ever see us again. Have you got that? It's just too too nauseating."

"Let me speak to your mother."

"No, this is my call. I'm paying for this. They're right here and they say it's my call. And they support me because they love me. That's the difference. My parents care about me. You just didn't care enough about Jeff. All you and Grandad ever thought about was yourselves, and that time you just left Jeff. . . ."

I couldn't speak. My heart was being bludgeoned. I hung up.

I was ill with doubt. Did I damage my son? Dear Goddess, what was the truth inside the poison?

There were no answers. There was no clarity. At three in the morning, I called Jeffrey and talked about nothing at all. A movie he'd seen. A friend who was visiting. My voice was high and bright and false. He couldn't know that tears were soaking through the sheets to the mattress.

"You sure it's just a cold, Mom? You sound different."

"I do?" I demonstrated my okayness with a little laugh and blew my nose. I tried to get my wavery voice under control.

Eleanor didn't call back when I left messages. "I've seen a doctor. Is that really what you wanted? All he's done is prescribe medication—which I'm not taking."

Charlie answered the phone one morning and hung up.

"This is too hard," I told Kate. "It's too unfair."

"Yes," she said. "It is too hard. It is unfair. But we don't know what they're going through. Don't call them. Call me."

After Charlie's hang-up, I didn't reach out again. I haven't spoken to Charlie or Eleanor or Cha Cha in five years. Cha Cha moved with a new partner to Los Angeles. Charlie and Eleanor followed. I wouldn't have known except for Kate, who heard indirectly through another friend. There are cards at Christmas from Eleanor, who signs Charlie's name, but there's nothing from Cha Cha.

Kate and I have talked about all this with less frequency over time, but the sadness never completely goes away. And so I cannot say that my life's great storm is ended, or that the story of Father is behind me. I cannot even say that the rainbow is a constant in my skies. But these days I experience friendship as life's great signature of hope, the pot at the end of the rainbow, the coinage of the abundant way. I do cherish my friends. Old friends, new friends. Kate. Lee Armitage. Constance Hobbs. As the familiar round goes,

> Make new friends but keep the old
> One is silver and the other gold.

Constance Hobbs's message of condolences one day was a warm embrace in a cold, dark season. Dear old Constance. She, who knew the closets and cupboards of my childhood home in a way that new friends could not, reconnected me to a magical childhood. She told me in our first conversation in decades, her voice still amazingly young, that she had moved back to Toronto when James became ill. He had died about three years earlier. Since then, she was back in demand at the Juniper Centres. What was I going to do? she asked. I didn't know.

In the end, thanks to Constance, it was the Juniper Centre here in Ontario that opened its northern woodsy sweet-smelling arms. The director, Dr. Lee Armitage, was a close friend of Kate's. She remembered me as Camper Songbird. "We have the space," Lee Armitage said, and welcomed not just me but the photographs, records, books, papers and "anything you'd like to bring." The entire staff signed a welcome card—Lee Armitage, Constance, Jane in the office, Doug who kept the grounds, Cookie who drove up from Chester Park every day. I looked steadfastly in the direction of welcome.

Kate laughed when I told her. "I know. I've been talking to Lee," she said. "Didn't I tell you, more things are wrought by friendship than this world dreams of?"

There was no time for careful sorting. The fireplace worked overtime. I packed Father's entire desk and contents, including the alabaster statue of Socrates. The piano, Lee Armitage said, they would particularly cherish. "It's an important part of our story." All the original songbooks went, the mountains of tapes from "Shelby Selects," some recorded workshops with the Hobbses.

The house was bought before it went in the listings, while the real estate man was arguing that the price was too low. I was in a hurry, I said, to sell.

The morning I left, the sky was dramatically black and white and blue. The crows leaned into the winds, sideways, backwards. Tree branches, wildly acrobatic, leapt in a thousand directions, the last few leaves flung loose in the chilly striptease.

Boots, in her carrying case in the back seat of the car,

cowered, hissing and growling her displeasure.

"Okay, Boots, okay. We're off."

I drove up to Juniper for one last goodbye—down the newly paved Main Street. The rectory was still there, hidden in the shadows behind pine trees now thick and higher than the roof. The old willow tree was gone. I parked in the alley, and looked up at my room, remembering the days when I would listen by the window for the sound of a car.

"Are you there, Stewart? Are you in the sound of the static?"

I know now that, although Stewart's love was a fiction in my adolescent mind, the Love that walks among us is more real than we are. In spite of all that happened when the scandal broke—the mudslinging, the family breakdown, the sadness of all the Brads and the Kelly Anns and the Jillys—throughout the long darkening I held to my hope. The Goddess of Mercy was the Goddess of Abundance. How triumphantly, how softly on the gentle feet of prayer, the declaration came to me that I was held, I was forgiven, I was being made whole, I was becoming free. I rested in this and I knew it to be sure. Now, today, I can say with the words of my clear trust that, even when utterly weak and lost and rejected, I was safe in the hands of the One who sees what I could not. This much, by faith, I do know. And to have come thus far is exhilarating.

Centuries ago, I'm told, in another world, in a place called Ellensburg, a minister called Martin Rinckart toiled in the hell of the Black Death. Within months, four and a half thousand people are said to have died. Martin Rinckart was conducting funerals. Fifty a day. One of the deaths was his wife's.

In that extremity, from the depths of the valley of the shadow, there came a mysterious and blazing and perhaps defiant light.

Martin Rinckart's great shout of thanksgiving endures.

> *Now thank we all our God with heart and hands and voices*
> *Who wondrous things hath done, in whom the world rejoices*
> *Who from our mothers' arms hath sent us on our way*
> *With countless gifts of love. . . .*

There are some who will conclude that Martin Rinckart was insane. But I think not. Suffering and evil are great mysteries. But so is love.

It is not, I have learned, the absence of night that creates the light. It is the gift of light received in the night; it is the attention of the light that creates our seeing.

I do not know how "countless gifts of love" from a "bounteous God" were apprehended by Martin Rinckart in the time of the Black Death. But it may be in the nature of sight that we can only see the brightest light when our world is most bleak. Glory, someone somewhere said, is what glows in the extremities of our experience.

I have no doubt that Martin Rinckart dwelt within the overwhelming evidence of Love's presence, and that he surrendered to it gladly. And it is even possible that my father, the thief of children's souls, received on his last Thanksgiving Day the light's reward. A thankful heart.

Many would be appalled to think that a man like Father could be the recipient of so great a gift. But perhaps it is not for us to know the workings of grace. For me it is enough to know that, as surely as night follows day and trial follows victory, there remains at all times a light that it is given us to glimpse. In a world such as ours, I would not ask for more than this.

CHAPTER THIRTY-TWO

At certain times of the day, especially in the early morning, the lake is the face of tranquillity. We have learned to pace ourselves throughout the intense summer and fall programmes with a few quiet days in between.

We are standing at the water's edge, Constance Hobbs, Lee Armitage and I, watching as the water creatures reveal themselves. Little slits of grey fish emerge—one, then two more, then still more. Small schools of slightly larger silvery fish criss-cross through the ripples. On the surface, skater insects, tiny catamarans, zap and pause on their long-legged stride past the white water lilies, past the dragonflies. A toothpick-thin black water snake quivers into view and disappears again.

Constance laments the diminishing worlds of songbirds, fireflies, butterflies, and the disappearance of the little green frogs, noting that the lake is being overrun by a new breed of bullfrogs, noisy and aggressive. We walk along the water's edge, old Boots sauntering along behind, as marble-size tadpoles, large black commas, plip and plop, rushing in their wriggly underwater race away from us.

Yesterday, the sun was particularly direct and hot. Lee and I came across Constance clambering naked down from a stone ledge and into the water. In her old age she is still tall and graceful, her breasts dangling, her long white hair a cloud around her angular shoulders.

"Why, Constance Elizabeth Hobbs!" Lee called, laughing delightedly and applauding.

"Come in, come in, you two!" Constance called back. "Hang your clothes on a hickory limb and—and. . . ."

"But don't go in the water?" Lee completed the nursery rhyme, and raised her eyebrows at me enquiringly. I shrugged. We peered nervously through the trees to make sure we really were the only ones around, and undressed self-consciously. Then, giggling like schoolgirls, we minced our way into the tingly cold of the startled lake.

We were about to come out when we were somewhat alarmed to hear a car, and moments later Donald Grantham, Lee's occasionally infuriating ex-husband, showed up.

"Aha!" he shouted as he came bounding down the path. He fiendishly made a lunge for our clothes, cackling that the three wicked witches were now in his power. Lee rose out of the water, a Venus de Milo, perfectly proportioned though not according to today's skeletal standards. "Out, out, out of my sight!" she shouted as she grabbed our garments from him, and Donald retreated sheepishly, his eyes feasting on his naked ex-wife. He is obviously still smitten by Lee, a classic beauty.

Donald Grantham and Lee Armitage both come from obscenely wealthy families. It's a good thing for the Juniper

Centres that they remain friends. We owe our basic existence to the benevolence of the Grantham Foundation, but it's the musical genius of Constance and James Hobbs that built the heady reputation of the Juniper Centres.

Donald Grantham is a great-nephew of Judge Grantham, the former United Church stalwart in Juniper who defected to our Anglican team and left his mansion and grounds to Father. Donald has been rather intent on securing the Grantham name for the Juniper Centres and refers to his great-uncle as the founder. He has revised history quite considerably, and Father's singular place is virtually gone from the literature. I have not objected. Nor has Charlie or anyone else. The truth that matters to me is not to be found in plaques or dedications or brochures. Of far greater value is the health that endures in the lives of those we leave behind. Constance agrees.

We spend much of our free time these days in the new Alice Grantham Morrison room, named after Donald's great-aunt, Judge Grantham's sister. Lee calls it the Great Grantham Ego room. It's a handsome space with a fireplace, dark oak book-shelves, a glass wall that looks out over a field of wildflowers. Our old piano shares the room with a new baby grand, and, like all musical instruments here, they are both lovingly maintained.

In the evenings, Constance and I often reminisce, lounging on the comfortable leather sofas and watching as the last embers in the fireplace flit and disappear. I've talked of Father's exquisite care of Mother in her last days. She's told me of James's long illness.

Earlier this spring, Lee, after one of her arguments with Donald, brought up the idea of an exhibition of the beginning of the Juniper Centres.

"You're the ones to do it," she said to Constance and me.

"Of course you are. You were both right there." And down we went to the storage room in the basement to look at the things I'd sent years before.

It's been a nostalgic summer. Along the east wall we have arranged a story line—a photograph of Judge Grantham in front of his mansion, and the rolling hills before anything else was built, the architect's drawings, some enlarged snapshots of the opening day, the parade and concert, the combined church and school choirs, excerpts from the article that made us famous and the first flyer announcing a concert featuring The Shelby Singers and the Hobbses.

These days we find ourselves sighing our way through a box of photographs that belong to Constance. There are several snapshots of Charlie and me that I hadn't seen before. One shows me on stage, my large alto recorder to my lips, my small hands stretched out over the instrument. For some reason, I'm looking cross-eyed. Then there's one of Charlie that stops my heart whenever I look at it. Charlie, about twelve, is gazing up at Father with unalloyed adoration and attention.

"A beautiful, beautiful boy," Constance said.

There is something in the way Charlie looks in the picture that reminds me of Jeffrey at that age. A certain purity of heart. An openness. Utter innocence. Two young boys. What do I know of what a young boy feels? My brother, my son. Here they were, suddenly interchangeable in my mind and walking into my heart through an old friend's old photographs. The many avenues of Love's walking. Love melting stones.

"Maybe Eleanor was right," I said. "Maybe it was harder for Charlie."

"Yes, it was, it was, Millicent. It broke his heart. I saw the change." She stood and went to the window. Even in her jogging outfit, Constance was regal. She looked out into the darkness. "How is he now? When did you last see him?"

"It's been years. Years and years."

"Some wounds take a long time. A lifetime. More than a lifetime."

"Or an instant."

Constance the healer turned to look at me, her moist eyes brimming. "Or an instant," she nodded. "Or an instant." She went to the old piano and sat playing softly for a few moments. "It may be just magical thinking on my part," she said, coming back and picking up Charlie's photo, "but I think that it's...."

I waited for her to finish her sentence. "It's?"

"Childhood. Such light." She shook her head. "How can one tell? How can one know? But my sense is—that the tenderness we feel at certain moments—these tiny tiny moments when the heart melts—when the heart opens—I think that moments like this, when we re-enter another time, a better time, a healing time—these are the world's most important moments. They're not heralded. They're not measured. They don't make headlines. But I do sense they affect the world immeasurably. I do think this, Millicent. When the heart opens, the light shines through."

CHAPTER THIRTY-THREE

It's another brilliant blue-sky Ontario and tall green trees everywhere morning. Clear. Crisp. A tiny mosquito bats itself against the screen.

I have waited so long—a lifetime—for this visit. I had expected to meet my curly-mopped little grandson years before, but life did not conspire to grant my fervent wish until this happiest month.

When he was about a year old, either Jeffrey left Lisa and the baby, or Lisa and the baby left Jeffrey. Jeffrey does not speak of that time. Perhaps Lisa had a need to discard the shadow of the Shelby skeleton. Their story has disappeared into the mists of England's countryside. I too had felt myself disappeared into the company of lost grandparents missing out of family albums, cut off from our baby-watching, story-telling years. All I had was the picture of a newborn in a birth announcement card—a tiny squinched-up muffin face in a hospital stocking cap. I searched the smudge for family resemblances.

Then, about two weeks ago, Constance and I were in the kitchen with some of last year's campers as we were waiting for a few stragglers to pick up their box lunches and join us for a hike. Constance was teaching a familiar round from my childhood that I hadn't heard in years and I was flooded with nostalgia. I was annoyed at the blaring interruption of the intercom.

"Long distance, Millicent." Everything was long distance here. The kitchen phone was on the wall beside the two refrigerators.

"Hello?" I heard Jane in the office hanging up.

"Hello, Mom?"

"My heavens! Jeffrey?" I turned to Constance. "It's Jeffrey! It's my son!"

"No!" Constance shook her head, her mouth open in amazement. She swung her guitar around to her back and quickly ushered the group outside.

"Jeffrey, where are you?"

He was calling from Toronto. He and Matty had just flown in, he said, and they were staying with an old school chum. They would be driving up to see me. My grandson wanted to meet his grandmother.

"See you in a few days," he said blithely.

I couldn't believe it. I was stunned.

"Mom. Are you there?"

"Tell me again, Jeff? What did you say?"

I hung up the phone and whooped and ran out to hug Constance.

Jeff and Matty arrived a week ago, driving up in a small truck complete with tent and sleeping bags and propane cooker. Constance, to give us a bit of privacy, reorganized the camp's plans and took the girls camping in the guest house by the waterfall. They all came back late last night.

The morning light whispers in now through the curtains, soft and salad-green and impish. Over by the campground in the trees, Matty, wearing his red Juniper Camp cap, is hopping about like a grasshopper with some of the other children. Not far from where the old wash house and cabins used to be, my blond lanky son, Jeffrey, so unlike his father, is squatting on the ground, leaning against a tree and droning into his seven-foot-long yidaki, an Australian aboriginal didjeridoo. He carved it out of a juniper tree years ago, when he was in Colorado at a music camp. The twenty-five-thousand-year-old primeval call thrums its ancient way through the air and into my room.

I open the window wider to let in the sound, to let in the sky. Matty sees me waving and is running this way. My grandchild. My own child's own sweet child. I step into my thongs and out through the sliding glass door onto the wraparound balcony, then lightly flap flap over the cool dew and down the steps to the gravelly path to greet him. Around us rises the fresh morning scent of the woods, the incense of the forest. Matty's arms are wide with welcome, as are mine. He'll probably want to go down to the lake again, as he does every morning, but I can't wait to show him off to Constance. I wonder if she's up. I wonder if she'll notice that his hair, thick and curly, is like mine. That was the first thing I saw when they arrived. Matty was asleep, zipped up in a sleeping bag. "Jeffrey," I gasped, "the hair!"

Jeffrey grinned and hugged me. "He's a Shelby, all right," he said.